PENGUIN BOOKS

The Street

Mordecai Richler's novels include *The Appren-ticeship of Duddy Kravitz, Cocksure, St. Urbain's Horse-man, Joshua Then and Now* and, most recently, the critically acclaimed *Solomon Gursky Was Here.* He has written the children's books *Jacob Two-Two Meets the Hooded Fang* and *Jacob Two-Two and the Dinosaur.* His essay collections include *Hunting Ti-gers Under Glass, Home Sweet Home,* and, most re-cently, *Broadsides.* He is also the editor of two an-thologies: *The Best of Modern Humour* and the re-cently published *Writers on World War II.* Rooted in London for twenty years, he returned to Canada with his wife and five children in 1972 and now divides his time between Montreal and a cottage in Quebec's Eastern Townships.

D0940823

the street

mordecai
richler

Penguin Books

PENGUIN BOOKS

Published by the Penguin Group
Penguin Books Canada Ltd, 10 Alcorn Avenue, Toronto, Ontario, Canada M4V 3B2
Penguin Books Ltd, 27 Wrights Lane, London W8 5TZ, England
Penguin Books USA Inc., 375 Hudson Street, New York, New York 10014, U.S.A.
Penguin Books Australia Ltd, Ringwood, Victoria, Australia
Penguin Books (NZ) Ltd, 182-190 Wairau Road, Auckland 10, New Zealand

Penguin Books Ltd, Registered Offices: Harmondsworth, Middlesex, England

First published in Canada by McClelland and Stewart Limited, 1969
First published in Penguin Books, 1977
Published in Penguin Books, this edition, 1985

3 5 7 9 10 8 6 4

Manufactured in Canada by Webcom Limited

Canadian Cataloguing in Publication Data
Richler, Mordecai, 1931-
The street

Originally published: Toronto: McClelland and
Stewart, 1969.
ISBN 0-14-015817-0

I. Title.

PS8535.I38S7 1991   C813'.54   C91-095096-2
PR9199.3.R5S7 1991

For Daniel, Noah, Emma,
Martha and Jacob

Most of these stories and memoirs first appeared, sometimes in a slightly different form, in *The New Statesman, Commentary,* the *Kenyon Review,* the *London Magazine, Canadian Literature* and *Macleans*, and I would like to thank the editors for permission to reprint them here. "Pinky's Squealer" (formerly titled "The Other Beach") is an excerpt from *Son of a Smaller Hero*.

M.R.

the street

Contents

Introduction

As a discipline, obviously the short story is more precise than the novel, not nearly so tolerant of literary truancies: digressions, self-indulgences. It strikes me as an unforgiving test, second only to poetry, of the ability to distill experience, and I am charged with admiration for writers who can do it well. But there is little justice to be had in this world. Or, put another way, in this country (as in others) more reverence is paid to novelists — a sloppy bunch — than to short story writers, even though some of the most satisfying work to be torn from the tundra has been delivered by our short story writers: say, Morley Callaghan, Alice Munro, Mavis Gallant. To compound the injury, readers — for reasons beyond my comprehension — will more readily fork out money for a novel than for a collection of short stories. So publishers are always badgering their short story writers to produce a novel. I imagine even Chekhov's publisher complained, "Anton, Anton, not yet another collection of such unmovable stuff. Look at Leo's sales. See how well that crazy Freddy is doing. Bring me the big one, kid."

Many years ago, a callow but ambitious nineteen-year-old, I started out as a would-be short story writer, intent on a classy career fed by an annual retainer from *The New Yorker*. But the only short story I ever sent them — from Ibiza, in 1951 — bounced back with a rejection slip. *The Atlantic*, *Harper's* and *Esquire* also returned my stories without a murmur of encouragement. I suppose I could have then tried dentistry or *The Canadian Forum*. But I wasn't going back to school, no sir, and publishing a story in the *Forum*, like winning a prize in a film festival in Regina or pitching a no-hitter in Red Deer, seemed to me more a confession of inadequacy than an accolade. So I made my first attempt at a novel, shrewdly calculating that it would not be neccessary for me to shine in every paragraph: instead, I might be pardoned pages of dross for the nuggets to be found here and there. Like the pitcher unable to throw sufficient red hot, I tried to develop a fork-ball, a little off-speed, a slo-mo sinker and other deceptive junk. I published my first novel *The Acrobats* in 1954, and have cunningly kept it out of print ever since. In a little book he once wrote about me, George Woodcock ventured that I had fled Canada after *The Acrobats* had been published to such punk reviews. Actually, I had quit Canada long before the novel was published, and had I elected to flee every country where it had been poorly received I would still be a travelling man.

Following *The Acrobats*, I tried my hand at short stories again. Alas, success in the form continued to elude me — and this is in the nature of a deeply felt complaint, because I still consider myself something of a failed short story writer. *The Apprenticeship of Duddy Kravitz*, for instance, began as an earnest short story about an embittered alcoholic high school teacher, Mr. MacPherson, and a young St. Urbain Street scamp called Duddy. I wrote it in Tourettes-sur-loup, high in the Alpes-Maritimes, only to have it turned down by *Com-*

mentary. Two years passed before I pulled it out of a drawer and set to work on it again. I was back in the south of France, blessed with a Junior Canada Council Grant which enabled me to spend my time turning Duddy into a novel and, less successfully, trying to extend my grant at the casino tables of Monte Carlo.

Cocksure was also rooted in a short story, one I actually managed to publish in *Tamarack Review*, titled "Mortimer Griffin, Shalinsky, and How They Settled the Jewish Question." And the same is true of *St. Urbain's Horseman*. The story didn't work, but the novel, like Topsy, just grew and grew. *Joshua Then and Now*, on the other hand, began as a text for a book of photographs of Spain. But when my wife read the text, she said, "This won't do for a travel book, but I think you have begun another novel." Which meant I was going to pick on her and the children for the rest of the day.

A sensible man, I will do anything to avoid writing novels, yet I sentence myself to it again and again only because I can't sing and I can't dance, I am unable to write poetry and have managed only a few short stories.

Here they are.

Most of the short stories I have ever published are included in this collection — a mixed bag, for it is also larded with a number of quasi-autobiographical memoirs, some journalism and vignettes. The stories in *The Street* were written over a period of ten years, between 1958 and 1968, and were first published in book form in Canada in 1969. Two years later they were published in England, tied to the tail of *St. Urbain's Horseman*, and in 1975 there was an American edition. Many of these vignettes first appeared in the *New Statesman*, and the receipt of my first cheque from that once legendary periodical, for twelve guineas, actually signed by Kingsley Martin, is a memory I still cherish. But the two stories I like best in this collection did not appear in the

Statesman. "The Summer My Grandmother was Supposed to Die" was first broadcast by the CBC and "Some Grist For Mervyn's Mill" was first published in *The Kenyon Review* and then in *Martha Foley's The Best American Short Stories 1963*.

None of the stories collected here are experimental or wildly original. Some are tainted by nostalgia, others strike me as slight. But they mapped out a territory, they staked a claim that would be more deeply mined in my novels. Certainly, I am pleased to have Penguin Books publish this new edition.

1984

Going Home Again

Going Home Again

"Why do you want to go to university?" the student counsellor asked me.

Without thinking, I replied, "I'm going to be a doctor, I suppose."

A doctor.

One St. Urbain Street day cribs and diapers were cruelly withdrawn and the next we were scrubbed and carted off to kindergarten. Though we didn't know it, we were already in pre-med school. School starting age was six, but fiercely competitive mothers would drag protesting four-year-olds to the registration desk and say, "He's short for his age."

"Birth certificate, please?"

"Lost in a fire."

On St. Urbain Street, a head start was all. Our mothers read us stories from *Life* about pimply astigmatic fourteen-year-olds who had already graduated from Harvard or who were confounding the professors at M.I.T. Reading *Tip-Top Comics* or listening to *The Green Hornet* on the radio was

as good as asking for a whack on the head, sometimes ad-
ministered with a rolled-up copy of *The Canadian Jewish
Eagle*, as if that in itself would be nourishing. We were not
supposed to memorise baseball batting averages or dirty
limericks. We were expected to improve our Word Power
with the *Reader's Digest* and find inspiration in Paul de
Kruif's medical biographies. If we didn't make doctors, we
were supposed to at least squeeze into dentistry. School
marks didn't count as much as rank. One wintry day I came
home, nostrils clinging together and ears burning cold,
proud of my report. "I came rank two, Maw."

"And who came rank one, may I ask?"

Mrs. Klinger's boy, alas. Already the phone was ringing.
"Yes, yes," my mother said to Mrs. Klinger, "congratulations,
and what does the eye doctor say about your Riva, poor kid,
to have a complex at her age, will they be able to straighten
them . . ."

Parochial school was a mixed pleasure. The old, underpaid men who taught us Hebrew tended to be surly, im-
patient. Ear-twisters and knuckle-rappers. They didn't like
children. But the girls who handled the English-language
part of our studies were charming, bracingly modern and
concerned about our future. They told us about *El Campe-
sino*, how John Steinbeck wrote the truth, and read Sacco's
speech to the court aloud to us. If one of the younger, un-
married teachers started out the morning looking weary we
assured each other that she had done it the night before.
Maybe with a soldier. Bareback.

From parochial school, I went on to a place I call Flet-
cher's Field High in the stories and memoirs that follow.
Fletcher's Field High was under the jurisdiction of the
Montreal Protestant School Board, but had a student body
that was nevertheless almost a hundred per cent Jewish.
The school became something of a legend in our area.
Everybody, it seemed, had passed through FFHS. Canada's

most famous gambler. An atom bomb spy. Boys who went off to fight in the Spanish Civil War. Miracle-making doctors and silver-tongued lawyers. Boxers. Fighters for Israel. All of whom were instructed, as I was, to be staunch and bold, to play the man, and, above all, to

> Strive hard and work
> With your heart in the doing.
> Up play the game,
> As you learnt it at Fletcher's.

Again and again we led Quebec province in the junior matriculation results. This was galling to the communists amongst us who held we were the same as everyone else, but to the many more who knew that for all seasons there was nothing like a Yiddish boy, it was an annual cause for celebration. Our class at FFHS, Room 41, was one of the few to boast a true Gentile, an authentic white Protestant. Yugoslavs and Bulgarians, who were as foxy as we were, their potato-filled mothers sitting just as rigid in their corsets at school concerts, fathers equally prone to natty straw hats and cursing in the mother-tongue, did not count. Our very own WASP's name was Whelan, and he was no less than perfect. Actually blond, with real blue eyes, and a tendency to sit with his mouth hanging open. A natural hockey player, a born first-baseman. Envious students came from other classrooms to look him over and put questions to him. Whelan, as was to be expected, was not excessively bright, but he gave Room 41 a certain tone, some badly needed glamour, and in order to keep him with us as we progressed from grade to grade, we wrote essays for him and slipped him answers at examination time. We were enormously proud of Whelan.

Among our young school masters, most of them returned war veterans, there were a number of truly dedicated men as well as some sour and brutish ones, like Shaw, who strapped twelve of us one afternoon, ten on each hand, because we wouldn't say who had farted while his back was turned. The foibles of older teachers were well-known to us, because so many aunts, uncles, cousins and elder brothers had preceded us at FFHS. There was, for instance, one master who initiated first year students with a standing joke. "Do you know how the Jews make an 's'?"

"No, Sir."

Then he would make an 's' on the blackboard and draw two strokes through it. The dollar sign.

Among us, at FFHS, were future leaders of the community. Progressive parents. Reform-minded aldermen. Anti-fallout enthusiasts. Collectors of early French Canadian furniture. Boys who would actually grow up to be doctors and lecture on early cancer warnings to ladies' clubs. Girls who would appear in the social pages of the Montreal *Star*, sponsoring concerts in aid of retarded children (regardless of race, colour, or creed) and luncheon hour fashion shows, proceeds to the Hebrew University. Lawyers. Notaries. Professors. And marvelously with-it rabbis, who could not only quote Rabbi Akiba but could also get a kick out of a hockey game. But at the time who would have known that such slouchy, aggressive girls, their very brassieres filled with bluff, would grow up to look so serene, such honeys, seeking apotheosis at the Saidye Bronfman Cultural Centre, posing on curving marble stairwells in their bouffant hair styles and strapless gowns? Or that such nervy boys, each one a hustler, would mature into men who were so damn pleased with what this world has to offer, epiphanous, radiating self-confidence at the curling or country club, at ease even with pot-bellies spilling over their Bermuda shorts? Who would have guessed?

Not me.

Looking back on those raw formative years at FFHS, I must say we were not a promising or engaging bunch. We were scruffy and spiteful, with an eye on the main chance. So I can forgive everybody but the idiot, personally unknown to me, who compiled our criminally dull English reader of prose and poetry. Nothing could have been calculated to make us hate literature more unless it was being ordered, as a punishment, to write *Ode To The West Wind* twenty-five times. And we suffered that too.

Graduation from FFHS meant jobs for most of us, McGill for the annointed few, and the end of an all but self-contained world made up of five streets, Clark, St. Urbain, Waverley, Esplanade, and Jeanne Mance, bounded by the Main, on one side, and Park Avenue, on the other.

By 1948 the drift to the suburbs had begun in earnest.

Flying into Montreal nineteen years later, in the summer of 1967, our very golden Expo summer, coming from dowdy London, via decaying New York, I was instantly struck by the city's affluence. As our jet dipped toward Dorval, I saw what appeared to be an endless glitter of eccentrically shaped green ink wells. Suburban swimming pools. For Arty and Stan, Zelda, Pinky's Squealer, Nate, Fanny, Shloime, and Mrs. Klinger's rank-one boy; all the urchins who had learnt to do the dead man's float with me in the winding muddy Shawbridge river, condemned by the health board each August as a polio threat.

I rode into the city on multi-decked highways, which swooped here, soared there, unwinding into a pot of prosperity, a downtown of high rise apartments and hotels, the latter seemingly so new they could have been uncrated the night before.

Place Ville Marie. The metro. Expo. Ile Notre Dame. Habitat. Place des Arts. This cornucopia certainly wasn't the city I had grown up in and quit.

Amidst such unnerving strangeness, I desperately sought reassurance in the familiar, the *Gazette* and the *Star*, turning

at once to that zingy, harmlessly inane duo. Fitz and Bruce
Taylor, the columnists who after all these testing years are
still the unchallenged Keepers of Ourtown's Social Record.
Should planets collide, nuclear warfare rage, I could still
count on this irrepressible pair to bring me up-to-date on my
old schoolmates, telling me which one, now a mutual funds
salesman with a split-level in Hampstead, had just shot a
hole-in-one in Miami; how many, as thickened round the
middle as I am, had taken to jogging at the 'y'; and if any,
prematurely taken by a coronary or ostensibly recuperating
from a lung removal operation, would be sorely missed by
the sporting crowd, not to say their Pythian lodge brothers.

Fitz and Taylor did not let me down, but I was brought
up short by an item which announced a forthcoming radio
programme, *Keep Off The Grass*, wherein local savants,
suburban cops and plainclothes teachers, would warn the
kids against pot.

Pot.

For the record, pot, like the *Reader's Digest*, is not
necessarily habit-forming, but both can lead to hard-core
addiction: heroin, in one case, abridged bad books, in the
other. Either way you look at it, a withdrawal from a meaningful life.

In our St. Urbain Street time, however, the forbidden food
had been ham or lobster and when we had objected, protesting it wasn't habit-forming, our grandfathers, faces flaring
red, had assured us if you start by eating pig, if you stray so
far from tradition, what next? Where will it end? And so
now we know. With the children's children smoking pot,
making bad trips, discovered stoned in crash pads.

Expo was of course thoroughly exhilarating and my wife
and I decided to return to Montreal and try it for a year, not
so much new as retreaded Canadians. We arrived in Sep-
tember 1968, picking, as it now turns out, a winter to try
men's souls. Dr. Johnson has described this country as "a

region of desolate sterility . . . a cold, uncomfortable, uninviting region, from which nothing but furs and fish were to be had." More recently, W. H. Auden has written, "The dominions . . . are for me *tiefste Provinz*, places which have produced no art and are inhabited by the kind of person with whom I have least in common."

Unfair comment without question, but I had only been back a month or so when I read PENSIONER FLUNKS TEST IN MONTREAL'S LOTTERY, thereby missing out on a possible one hundred thousand dollar jackpot.

A half-blind disability pensioner yesterday became the first contestant to flunk Mayor Jean Drapeau's voluntary tax non-lottery . . . when he failed to name Paris as the largest French-speaking city . . .

This, to a sometime satirist, was meaty stuff indeed. A repast unbelievably enhanced when I read on to discover that our cunning, indefatigable mayor, possibly generalising from the particular of the city council, had commented: "This proves the questions are not easy, and that they are a real test of skill."

O God! O Montreal! now branded by its mayor as the metropolis wherein recognition of Paris as the world's largest French-speaking city is taken as a measure of intellectual fallibility.

And hippies are hounded as plague-bearers.

Possibly, the problem is I was raised to manhood in a hairier, more earthy Montreal, the incomparable Mayor Camellien Houde's canton, whose troubles were basically old-fashioned, breaking down into the pleb's too large appetite for barbotte tables and whore houses. At the time, Montreal endured a puritanical avenger as well as a journalist champion of the permissive society. All-seeing Police Commissioner 'Pax' Plante, scourge of harlots, implacable enemy of bookies with something hot on the morning line, raked the debauched streets in a black limousine, a sort of French Canadian batman. On the other hand, Al Palmer, with the now-defunct *Herald*, campaigned intrepidly for our right to buy margarine *over the counter* – margarine once as illicit in Quebec province as marijuana is today. Al Palmer who was, in his time, the Dr. Tim Leary of artificial foods.

In those days, it should be remembered, no cop would have ventured, as did Detective-Sergeant Roger Lavigueur at a recent policemen's union meeting, to threaten us with a *coup d'état*, saying, "It happens every day in South America. It could happen here too. We, the policemen, may have to take over the government."

In the civilized Forties, before Marcuse, Fanon, Ché, and Mayor Daley, our cops, civic and provincial, never split a head unless it was rockhard – that is to say, a striker's head. Otherwise they were so good-natured that before raiding a gambling den or brothel they phoned to make sure nobody nice would be there and, on arrival, resolutely padlocked the toilet and picked up a little something for their trouble on the way out.

In the immediate post-war years hippies need not have cadged off unemployment insurance, inflaming Ourtown's over-achievers, but instead could have survived and served the straight community as well by voting, as did many an inner-directed St. Urbain Street boy, twenty or more times in any civic, provincial or federal election. These, remember, were the roseate years when commie traitor Fred Rose, our M.P., went from parliament to prison and was replaced by Maurice Hartt of whom *Time* wrote:

> Hartt's principal campaign asset is his whiplash tongue, which he has used on many an opponent. Once he so angered Premier Duplessis in the legislature with

an attack on him that the livid Premier called to Liberal
Leader Adélard Godbout: "Have you another Jew in this
House to speak for you?" Hartt bounded up, pointed to
the crucifix behind the Speaker's chair and cried: "Yes,
you have – His image has been speaking to you for 2,000
years, but you still don't understand Him."

A time when many a freshly-scrubbed young notary was
elected to the city council for a dollar a year and, lo and
behold, emerged one or two terms later a real estate million-
aire, lucky enough to hold the rocky farmlands where new
highways were to be built or schools constructed. This arche-
typal city councillor, now just possibly a church or synagogue board chairman, certainly a Centennial Medal holder,
is the man most likely to inveigh against today's immoral
youngsters, kids so deficient in industry that far from voting
twenty times they don't go to the polls at all, or respect their
parents who grew up when a dollar was a dollar, dammit,
and to make one you hustled, leading with the elbows.

To come home in 1968 was to discover that it wasn't where
I had left it – it had been bulldozed away – or had become,
as is the case with St. Urbain, a Greek preserve.

Today the original Young Israel synagogue, where we
used to chin the bar, is no longer there. A bank stands where
my old poolroom used to be. Some of the familiar stores
have gone. There have been deaths and bankruptcies. But
most of the departed have simply packed up and moved with
their old customers to the new shopping centres at Van
Horne or Rockland, Westmount or Ville Ste Laurent.

Up and down the Main you can still pick out many of the
old restaurants and steak houses wedged between the sweater factories, poolrooms, cold-water flats, wholesale dry goods
stores, and "Your Most Sanitary" barbershops. The places
where we used to work in summer as shippers for ten dollars

a week are still there. So is Fletcher's Field High, right where
it always was. Rabbinical students and boys with sidecurls
still pass. These, however, are the latest arrivals from Poland
and Rumania and soon their immigrant parents will put
pressure on them to study hard and make good. To get out.

But many of our grandparents, the very same people who
assured us the Main was only for *bummers* and failures, will
not get out. Today when most of the children have made
good, now that the sons and daughters have split-level
bungalows and minks and West Indian cruises in winter,
many of the grandparents still cling to the Main. Their children cannot in many cases persuade them to leave. So you
still see them there, drained and used up by the struggle.
They sit on kitchen chairs next to the coke freezer in the
cigar store, dozing with a fly swatter held in a mottled hand.
You find them rolling their own cigarettes and studying the
obituary columns in the *Star* on the steps outside the Jewish
Library. The women still peel potatoes under the shade of a
winding outside staircase. Old men still watch the comings
and goings from the balcony above, a blanket spread over
their legs and a litle bag of polly seeds on their lap. As in the
old days the sinking house with the crooked floor is right over
the store or the wholesaler's, or maybe next door to the scrap
yard. Only today the store and the junk yard are shut down.
Signs for Sweet Caporal cigarettes or old election posters
have been nailed in over the missing windows. There are
spider webs everywhere.

The Street

The Street

In 1953, on the first Sunday after my return to Montreal from a two year stay in Europe, I went to my grandmother's house on Jeanne Mance street.

A Yiddish newspaper fluttering on her massive lap, black bootlaces unravelled, my grandmother was ensconced in a kitchen chair on the balcony, seemingly rooted there, attended by sons and daughters, fortified by grandchildren. "How is it for the Jews in Europe?" she asked me.

A direct question from an old lady with a wart turned like a screw in her cheek and in an instant I was shorn of all my desperately acquired sophistication; my *New Statesman* outlook, my shaky knowledge of wines and European capitals; the life I had made for myself beyond the ghetto.

"I don't know," I said, my shame mixed with resentment at being reclaimed so quickly. "I didn't meet many."

Leaning against their shiny new cars, yawning on the balcony steps with hands thrust into their trouser pockets or munching watermelon, pinging seeds into saucers, my uncles reproached me for not having been to Israel. But their questions about Europe were less poignant than my grandmother's. Had I seen the Folies Bergères? The changing of the guards? My uncles had become Canadians.

Canada, from the beginning, was second-best. It made us nearly Americans.

My grandfather, like so many others, ventured to Canada by steerage from a Gallician *shtetl*, in 1904, following hard on the outbreak of the Russo-Japanese War and the singularly vile pogrom in Kishinev, which was instigated by the militant anti-semite P. A. Krushevan, editor of *Znamya (The Banner)*, who four months later was the first to publish in Russia the *Minutes of the Meeting of the World Union of Freemasons and Elders of Zion*, which he called *Programme for World Conquest by the Jews*.

My grandfather, I was astonished to discover many years later, had actually had a train ticket to Chicago in his pocket. Canada was not a choice, but an accident. On board ship my grandfather encountered a follower of the same hasidic rabbi; the man had a train ticket to Montreal, but relatives in Chicago. My grandfather knew somebody's cousin in Toronto, also in Canada, he was informed. So the two men swapped train tickets on deck one morning.

On arrival in Montreal my grandfather acquired a peddler's licence and a small loan from the Baron de Hirsch Institute and dug in not far from the Main Street in what was to become a ghetto. Here, as in the real America, the immigrants worked under appalling conditions in sweatshops. They rented halls over poolrooms and grocery stores to meet and form burial societies and create *shuls*. They sent to the old country for younger brothers and cousins left behind, for rabbis and brides. Slowly, unfalteringly, the immigrants began to struggle up a ladder of streets, from one where you had to leave your garbage outside your front door to another where you actually had a rear lane as well as a back yard where corn and tomatoes were usually grown; from the three rooms over the fruit store or tailor shop to your own cold-water flat. A street with trees.

Our street was called St. Urbain. French for Urban. Actually there have been eight popes named Urban, but ours was the first. Urban 1. He was also the only one to have been canonized.

St. Urbain ultimately led to routes 11 and 18, and all day and night big refrigeration trucks and peddlers in rattling chevvies and sometimes tourists used to pass, hurtling to and from northern Quebec, Ontario, and New York State. Occasionally the truckers and peddlers would pull up at Tansky's for a bite.

"Montreal's a fine town," they'd say. "Wide open."

Unfailingly, one of the truckers would reply, "It's the Gay Paree of North America."

But if the trucker or peddler was from Toronto, he would add, ingratiatingly, "The only good thing about Toronto is the road to Montreal. Isn't that so?"

The regulars at Tansky's felt it was a good omen that the truckers and peddlers sometimes stopped there. "They know the best places," Segal said.

Some of the truckers had tattoos on their arms, others chewed tobacco or rolled their own cigarettes with Old Chum. The regulars would whisper about them in Yiddish.

"I wonder how long *that* one's been out of prison?"

"The one with all the holes in his face smells like he hasn't changed his underwear since God knows when."

The truckers struck matches against the seat of their shiny trousers or by flicking them with a thumbnail. They could spit on the floor with such a splash of assurance that it was the regulars who ended up feeling like intruders in Tansky's Cigar & Soda.

"I'll bet you the one with the ears can't count to twenty without taking his shoes off."

"But you don't understand," Takifman, nodding, sucking mournfully on an inverted pipe, would reassure them. "Statistics prove they're happier than we are. They care their kids should go to the McGill? They have one every nine months regular as clock-work. Why? For the family allowance cheque."

When the regulars carried on like that, belittling the bigger, more masculine men, Tansky would regard them reproachfully. He would put out delicate little feelers to the truckers. His brothers, the French Canadians. Vanquished, oppressed.

Peering over the rim of his glasses, Tansky would say, "Isn't it a shame about the strikers in Granby?" Or looking up from his newspaper, pausing to wet a thumb, he'd try, "And what about our brothers, the blacks?"

Then he would settle back and wait.

If one of the truckers replied, "It's shit, everything's shit," and the other sneered, "I try to mind my own business, buster," Tansky's shaggy grey head would drop and he would have to be reminded to add mustard and relish to the hamburgers. But if the truckers were responsive or, more likely, shrewd, if one said, "It's the system," and the other, "Maybe after the war things will be different," they would earn heaping plates of french fried potatoes and complimentary refills of coffee.

"It's one hell of a life," one of the truckers might say and Tansky would reply fervently, "We can change it. It's up to the people."

Even in winter the regulars used to risk the wind and the ice to slip outside and stamp up and down around the enormous trailer trucks, reminding each other that they too could have been millionaires today, fabled philanthropists, sought-after community leaders, if only, during prohibition, they too had been willing to bootleg, running booze over the border in trucks like these.

Another opportunity missed.

Looking in here, landing a little slap there, the regulars always stopped to give the tires a melancholy kick.

"You should have what one of these babies burns in gas in one night."

"Ach. It's no life for a family man."

It was different with the peddlers. Most of them were, as Miller put it, members of the tribe. Even if a man was so stupid, such a *putz*, that he couldn't tell from their faces or if – like Tansky, perhaps – he indignantly held that there was no such thing as a Jewish face, he still knew because before the peddlers even sat down for a coffee they generally phoned home and looked to see if Tansky sold pennants or toys to take back as a memento for the kids. They didn't waste time, either. They zipped through their order book as they ate, biting their pencils, adding, subtracting, muttering to themselves, and if they were carrying an item that Tansky might feasibly use they tried to push a sale right there. If not, they would offer the regulars cut-rates on suits or kitchen ware. Some of the peddlers were kidders and carried come-ons with them to entice the French Canadian hicks in Ste Jerome and Trois-Rivières, Tadoussac and Restigouche. Hold a key chain socket to your eye and see a naked cutie wiggle. Pour seltzer into a tumbler with a print of a girl on the side and watch her panties peel off.

Segal told all the peddlers the same joke, ruining it, as he did all his stories, by revealing the punch-line first. "Do you know the one," he'd say, "that goes Bloomberg's dead?"

"No. Well, I don't think so."

So Segal, quaking with laughter, would plunge into the story about this traveller, one of ours, a man called Bloomberg, who had a cock bigger than a Coorsh's salami. Built stronger than Farber the iceman's horse, let me tell you. He went from town to town, selling bolts of cloth, seconds, and banging *shiksas* (nuns included) on the cot in the back of his van, until the day he died. Another salesman, Motka Frish, was also in this godforsaken mining town in Labrador when he died. Motka hurried to the mortuary where the legendary Bloomberg lay on a slab and sliced off his cock, his unbelievably large member, to bring home and show to his wife, because otherwise, he thought, she would never believe a man could be so well hung. He returns home, unwraps the cock, and before he can get a word out, his wife has a peek and begins to pull her hair and wail. "Bloomberg's dead," she howls. "Bloomberg's dead."

Afterwards, still spilling with laughter, Segal would ask, "Heard any hot ones yourself lately?"

Takifman was another one who always had a word with the peddlers. "How is it," he would ask, already tearful, "for the Jews in Valleyfield?"

Or if the peddler had just come from Albany it was, "I hear the mayor there is an anti-semite."

"Aren't they all?"

"Not LaGuardia. LaGuardia of New York is A-1."

The peddlers would usually ask for a couple of dollars in silver and retreat to the phone booth for a while before they left.

Tansky's beat-up brown phone booth was an institution in our neighbourhood. Many who didn't have phones of their own used it to summon the doctor. "I'd rather pay a nickel here than be indebted to that cockroach downstairs for the rest of my life." Others needed the booth if they had a surreptitious little deal to transact or if it was the sabbath and they couldn't use their own phones because they had a father from the stone ages. If you had a party line you didn't dare use the phone in your own house to call the free loan society or the exterminator. Boys who wanted privacy used the phone to call their girl friends, though the regulars were particularly hard on them.

Between two and four in the afternoon the horse players held a monopoly on the phone. One of them, Sonny Markowitz, got an incoming call daily at three. Nat always took it for him. "Good afternoon," he'd say "Morrow Real Estate. Mr. Morrow. One moment, please."

Markowitz would grab the receiver, his manner breathless. "Glad you called, honey. But I've got an important client with me right now. Yes, doll. You bet. Soon as I can. *Hasta la vista*."

Anxious callers had long ago picked the paint off one wall of the booth. Others had scratched obscenities into the exposed zinc. Somebody who had been unable to get a date with Molly had used a key to cut MOLLY BANGS into the wall. Underneath, Manny had written ME TOO, adding his phone number. Doodles tended toward the expansively pornographic, they were boastful too, and most of the graffiti was obvious. KILROY WAS HERE. OPEN UP A SECOND FRONT. PERLMAN'S A SHVANTZ.

After each fight with Joey, Sadie swept in sobbing, hysterical, her housecoat fluttering. She never bothered to lower her voice. "It's happened again, Maw. No, he wasn't wearing anything. He wouldn't. Sure I told him what the doctor said. *I told him*. He said what are you, the B'nai Jacob Synagogue, I can't come in without wearing a hat? How do I know? I'm telling you, Maw, he's a beast, I want to come home to you. *That's not true*. I couldn't stop him if I wanted to. Yes, I washed before Seymour. A lot of good it does. All right, Maw. I'll tell him."

Sugarman never shuffled into Tansky's without first trying the slot in the booth to see if anyone had left a nickel behind. The regulars seldom paid for a call. They would dial their homes or businesses, ring twice, hang up, and wait for the return call.

Tansky's was not the only store of its sort on St. Urbain. Immediately across the street was Myerson's.

Myerson had put in cushions for the card players, he sold some items cheaper than Tansky, but he was considered to be a sour type, a regular snake, and so he did not do too well. He had his regulars, it's true, and there was some drifting to and fro between the stores out of pique, but if a trucker or a peddler stopped at Myerson's it was an accident.

Myerson had a tendency to stand outside, sweeping up with vicious strokes, and hollering at the men as they filed into Tansky's. "Hey, why don't you come over here for once? I won't bite you. Blood poisoning I don't need."

Myerson's rage fed on the refugees who began to settle on St. Urbain during the war years. "If they come in it's for a street direction," he'd say, "or if it's for a coke they want a dozen glasses with." He wasn't kind to kids. "You know what you are," he was fond of saying, "your father's mistake."

If we came in to collect on empty bottles, he'd say, "We don't deal in stolen goods here. Try Tansky's."

We enjoyed the excitement of the passing peddlers and truckers on St. Urbain – it was, as Sugarman said, an education – but we also had our traffic accidents. Once a boy was killed. An only son. Another time an old man. But complain, complain, we could not get them to install traffic lights on our corner.

"When one of ours is killed by a car they care? It saves them some dirty work."

But Tansky insisted it wasn't anti-semitism. Ours was a working-class area. That's why we didn't count.

St. Urbain was one of five working-class ghetto streets between the Main and Park Avenue.

To a middle-class stranger, it's true, the five streets would have seemed interchangeable. On each corner a cigar store, a grocery, and a fruit man. Outside staircases everywhere. Winding ones, wooden ones, rusty and risky ones. An endless repetition of precious peeling balconies and waste lots making the occasional gap here and there. But, as we boys knew, each street between the Main and Park Avenue represented subtle differences in income. No two cold-water flats were alike and no two stores were the same either. Best Fruit gypped on weight but Smiley's didn't give credit.

Of the five streets, St. Urbain was the best. Those on the streets below, the out-of-breath ones, the borrowers, the *yentas*, flea-carriers and rent-skippers, *goniffs* from Galicia, couldn't afford a day in the country or tinned fruit for dessert on the High Holidays. They accepted parcels from charity matrons (Outremont bitches) on Passover, and went uninvited to bar-mitzvahs and weddings to carry off cakes, bottles, and chicken legs. Their English was not as good as ours. In fact, they were not yet Canadians. *Greeners*, that's what they were. On the streets above, you got the ambitious ones. The schemers and the hat-tippers. The *pusherkes*.

Among the wonders of St. Urbain, our St. Urbain, there was a man who ran for alderman on a one-plank platform – provincial speed cops were anti-semites. There was a semi-pro whore, Cross-Eyed Yetta, and a gifted cripple, Pomerantz, who had had a poem published in *transition* before he shrivelled and died at the age of twenty-seven. There were two men who had served with the Mackenzie-Paps in the Spanish Civil War and a girl who had met Danny Kaye in the Catskills. A boy nobody remembered who went on to become a professor at m.i.t. Dicky Rubin who married a *shiksa* in the Unitarian Church. A Boxer who once made the *Ring* magazine ratings. Lazar of Best Grade Fruit who raked in twenty-five hundred dollars for being knocked down by a No. 43 streetcar. Herscovitch's nephew Larry who went to prison for yielding military secrets to Russia. A woman who actually called herself a divorcée. A man, A.D.'s father, who was bad luck to have in your house. And more, many more.

St. Urbain was, I suppose, somewhat similar to ghetto streets in New York and Chicago. There were a number of crucial differences, however. We were Canadians, therefore we had a King. We also had "pea-soups", that is to say, French Canadians, in the neighbourhood. While the King never actually stopped on St. Urbain, he did pass a few streets above on his visit to Canada just before the war. We were turned out of school to wave at him on our first unscheduled holiday, as I recall it, since Buster Crabbe, the Tarzan of his day, had spoken to us on Canada Youth Day.

"He looks to me *eppes*, a little pasty," Mrs. Takifman said.

My friends and I used to set pennies down on the tracks to be flattened by passing freight trains. Later, we would con the rich kids in Outremont, telling them that the Royal Train had gone over the pennies. We got a nickel each for them.

Earlier, the Prince of Wales came to Canada. He appeared at a Mizrachi meeting and my mother became one of thousands upon thousands who actually shook hands with him. When he abdicated the throne, she revealed, "Even then you could tell he was a romantic man. You could see it in his eyes."

"He has two," my father said, "just like me."

"Sure. That's right. You sacrifice a throne for a lady's love. It kills you to even give up a seat on the streetcar."

A St. Urbain street lady, Mrs. Miller of Miller's Home Bakery, made an enormous *chaleh*, the biggest loaf we had ever seen, and sent it to Buckingham Palace in time for Princess Elizabeth's birthday. A thank you note came from the Palace and Mrs. Miller's picture was in all the newspapers. "For local distribution," she told reporters, "we also bake knishes and cater for quality weddings."

Our attitude toward the Royal Family was characterized by an amused benevolence. They didn't affect the price of potatoes. Neither could they help or hinder the establishment of the State of Israel. Like Churchill, for instance. King George vi, we were assured, was just a figurehead. We could afford to be patronizing for among our kings we could count Solomon and David. True, we had enjoyed Bette Davis in

Elizabeth and Essex. We were flattered when Manny became a King's Scout. Why, we even wished the Royal Family a long life every Saturday in the synagogue, but this wasn't servility. It was generosity. Badly misplaced generosity when I recall that we also included John Buchan, 1st Lord Tweedsmuir of Elsfield, Governor-General of Canada, in our prayers.

As a boy I was enjoined by my school masters to revere John Buchan. Before he came to speak at Junior Red Cross Prize Day, we were told that he stood for the ultimate British virtues. Fair play, clean living, gentlemanly conduct. We were not forewarned that he was also a virulent anti-semite. I discovered this for myself, reading *The Thirty-Nine Steps.* I was scarcely into the novel, when I was introduced to Scudder, the brave and good spy, whom Richard Hannay takes to be "a sharp, restless fellow, who always wanted to get down to the root of things." Scudder tells Hannay that behind all governments and the armies there was a big subterranean movement going on, engineered by a very dangerous people. Most of them were the sort of educated anarchists that make revolutions, but beside them there were financiers who were playing for money. It suited the books of both classes of conspirators to set Europe by the ears:

> When I asked Why, he said that the anarchist lot thought it would give them their chance . . . they looked to see a new world emerge. The capitalists would . . . make fortunes by buying up the wreckage. Capital, he said, had no conscience and no fatherland. Besides, the Jew was behind it, and the Jew hated Russia worse than hell.
>
> 'Do you wonder?' he cried. 'For three hundred years they have been persecuted, and this is the return match for the *pogroms*. The Jew is everywhere, but you have to go far down the backstairs to meet him. Take any big Teutonic business concern. If you have dealings with it

the first man you meet is Prince *von und zu* Something,
an elegant young man who talks Eton-and-Harrow English. But he cuts no ice. If your business is big, you get
behind him and find a prognathous Westphalian with
retreating brow and the manners of a hog . . . But if you're
on the biggest kind of job and are bound to get to the
real boss, ten to one you are brought up against a little
white-faced Jew in a bathchair with an eye like a rattle
snake. Yes, sir, he is the man who is ruling the world just
now, and he has his knife in the Empire of the Tzar,
because his aunt was outraged and his father flogged in
some one-horse location on the Volga.'

As badly as I wanted to identify with Hannay, two-fisted
soldier of fortunte, I couldn't without betraying myself. My
grandfather, *pace* Buchan, had gone in fear of being flogged
in some one-horse location on the Volga, which was why we
were in Canada. However, I owe to Buchan the image of my
grandfather as a little white-faced Jew with an eye like a
rattlesnake. It is an image I briefly responded to, alas, if only
because Hannay, so obviously on the side of the good and the
clean, accepted it without question.

In those days British and American influences still vied
for our attention. We suffered split loyalties. I would have
liked, for instance, to have seen Tommy Farr pulverize Joe
Louis. We were enormously grateful when Donald Wolfit
came to town with a shambles of a Shakespearian company
and we applauded and stamped our feet for George Formby
at the Forum. Our best-known writers, Leacock, Hugh Mac-
Lennan and Robertson Davies, were clearly within a British
tradition. Our dentist took the *Illustrated London News* and
we all read Beverly Baxter's syrupy reports in *Macleans*
about lords and ladies he had taken strawberries and champagne with.

Pea-soups were for turning the lights on and off on the

sabbath and running elevators and cleaning out chimneys and furnaces. They were, it was rumoured, ridden with T.B., rickets, and the syph. Their older women were for washing windows and waxing floors and the younger ones were for maids in the higher reaches of Outremont, working in factories, and making time with, if and when you had the chance. The French Canadians were our *schwartzes*.

Zabitsky, a feared man, said, "It's not very well known, but there's a tunnel that runs from the nunnery to the priesthouse. It isn't there in case of an air-raid, either."

Zabitsky also told us how an altar boy could make himself a bishop's favourite, that a nun's habit concealed pregnancy, and that there was a special orphanage for the priests' bastards in Ste. Jerome.

To all this Shapiro said, "Well, snatch-erly," my father agreed, and Segal, warming to the idea, suggested a new definition for bishopric.

But when I recall St. Urbain I do not think so much of the men as of my old companions there. The boys. Mostly, we just used to sit around on the outside staircases shooting the breeze.

"Knock, knock."

"Who's there?"

"Freda."

"Freda who?"

"Fre-da you. Five dollars for anyone else."

Our hero was Ziggy 'The Fireball' Freed, who was signed on by a Dodger scout at the age of eighteen, and was shipped out for seasoning with a Class 'D' team in Texas. Ziggy lasted only a season. "You think they'd give a Hebe a chance to pitch out there?" he asked. "Sure, in the ninth inning, with the bases loaded and none out, and their home-run slugger coming up to the plate, the manager would shout, 'Okay, Ziggy, it's your ball game now.'"

Our world was rigidly circumscribed. Outside, where

they ate wormy pork, beat the wives for openers, didn't care
a little finger if the children grew up to be doctors, we
seldom ventured, and then only fearfully. Our world, its
prizes and punishments, was entirely Jewish. Inside, God
would get us if we didn't say our prayers. You ate the last
scrap of meat on your plate because the children in Europe
were starving. If you got it right on your bar-mitzvah who
knows but the rich uncle might buy you a Parker 51 set.

In our world what we knew of the outside was it wasn't a
life-saver if it didn't have a hole in it. If you ate plenty of
carrots you would see better in the dark, like R.A.F. night-
fighters. Every Thursday night on Station CBM Fibber Mc-
Gee would open his marvelous closet. Joe was always gone
for a Dow. Never before had so many owed so much to so
few. V stood for Victory. Paul Lukas was watching out for us
on the Rhine. The sure road to success was to buy cheap and
sell dear. In real life Superman was only mild Clark Kent.
A Roosevelt only comes along once in a lifetime. Scratch the
best goy and you find the worst anti-semite.

After school we sat on the steps and talked about everything from A to Z.

"Why is it Tarzan never shits?"

"What about Wonder Woman?"

"She's a dame, you jerk. But there's Tarzan in the jungle,
week in and week out, and never once does he go to the
toilet. It's not true to life, that's all."

In summer we bought old car tubes from the garage for
a nickel and took them to the beaches with us. We made
scooters out of waste wood and roller skates stolen or picked
up at a junk yard. Used horseshoes nicked from the French
Canadian blacksmith served us for games of pitch-toss. A
sock stuffed with sawdust was good enough for touch foot-
ball. During the worst of the winter we built a chain of snow
fortresses on St. Urbain and battled, one side against another,
shouting, "Guadacanal! *Schweinhund!* Take that, you yellow

devil!" With regular hockey sticks and pieces of coal and copies of Macleans for shin-pads we played right out on the streets, breaking up whenever a car wanted to pass.

When we grew a little older, however, our big thrill was to watch Molly go by.

Almost everything came to a stop on St. Urbain when Molly turned the corner at six-oh-five on her way home from Susy's Smart Wear, where she typed letters and invoices and occasionally modelled garments for out-of-town buyers. The boys in the Laurier Billiard Academy would be drawn to the window, still holding their cues.

"Here she comes. Right on the dot."

"Hey, Molly. Molly, my darling. How would you like to try this for supper?"

High stiletto heels, long slender legs, and a swinging of hips. Lefty groans. "You shoulda been here yesterday."

"Wha'?"

"There was a breeze. She wears a black slip with itsy-bitsy frills."

Eyes crossed, tongue protruding, pool cue squeezed between his thighs, Jerry pretends to pull himself off.

"Hey," Morty says, "I'll bet you guys have no idea why they put saltpetre in your cigs in the army."

Down the street she drifts, trailing Lily of the Valley.

"You ever heard of this stuff called Spanish Fly? I'm not saying I believe it but Lou swears –"

"Aw, go home and squeeze your pimples out. It's the bull."

Across the street, toward Myerson's.

"Yeow! Take care, doll. Don't take chances with it."

Cars gearing down, windows rolling open.

"Here, pussy. Nice pussy."

"You dirty bastard," Myerson says, "take your hands out of your pocket."

"*All right.*"

Past Best Grade Fruit.

"You see this pineapple?"

"I dare you."

Molly stops – considers – stoops. A stocking seam is straightened.

"You know, Bernie, I'd give a year of my life – well maybe not a year, but – "

"The line forms at the right."

Tickety-tap, tickety-tap, she goes, bottom swaying.

Myrna raises an eyebrow. "If I was willing to wear a skirt as tight as that – "

"It's asking? It's *begging* for it," Gitel says.

" – I could have all the boys I wanted to."

At the Triangle Taxi Stand, Max Kravitz twists his cap around. "Up periscope," he says, raising his arms to adjust the imaginary instrument.

"Longitude zero," Korber says, "latitude 38-29-38. She carries twin stacks."

"Ach, so. A destroyer. Ready torpedoes."

"Ready torpedoes, men."

"Ready torpedoes," is shouted down the queue of waiting drivers. Cooper, the last man, calls back, "If you ask me all periscopes are already up and all torpedoes – "

"FIRE!"

A pause.

"*Nu?*"

"She's going down."

"Heil Hitler!"

Into Tansky's for a package of Sen-Sen, ten filter-tips, the latest issue of *Silver Screen*. Takifman adjusts his tie and Segal drops a mottled hand to make sure he's buttoned.

"If I was her father," Takifman says, "I'd turn her over for a good spanking before I let her go out on the streets like that."

"Me too," Segal agrees with appetite.

St. Urbain, we felt, was inviolable. Among us we numbered the rank-one scholars in the province, gifted artists, medical students, and everywhere you looked decent, God-fearing people. It was a little embarrassing admittedly, when Mrs. Boxer, the *meshugena*, wandered the streets in her nightgown singing Jesus Loves Me. Our landlords, by and large, were rotten types. Polacks, Bulgarians, and other trash were beginning to move in here and there. When that sweet young man from CHFD's "Vox Pop" asked Ginsburg, didn't he think Canada ought to have a flag of her own, he shouldn't have come back with, you do what you like, *we* already have a flag. Not on the radio, anyway. Sugarman's boy, Stanley, it's true, had had to do six months at Ste. Vincent de Paul for buying stolen goods, but all the time he was there he refused to eat non-kosher food. We had our faults on St. Urbain, but nobody could find anything truly important to criticise.

Then one black, thundering day there was an article about our street in *Time* magazine. For several years we had been electing communists to represent us at Ottawa and in the provincial legislature. Our M.P. was arrested. An atomic spy. *Time*, investigating the man's background in depth, described St. Urbain, our St. Urbain, as the Hell's Kitchen of Montreal. It brought up old election scandals and strikes and went into the housing question and concluded that this was the climate in which communism flourished.

The offending magazine was passed from hand to hand.

"What's 'squalor'?"

"*Shmutz.*"

"We're dirty? In my house you could eat off the floor."

"We're not poor. I can walk into any delicatessen in town, you name it, and order whatever my little heart desires."

"In our house there's always plenty for *shabbus*. I should show you my butcher's bills you'd die."

"This write-up's crazy. An insult."

"Slander, you mean. We ought to get Lubin to take the case."

"Ignoramous. You don't bring in ambulance-chasers to fight a case like this. You need one of theirs, a big-shot."

"What about Rosenberg? He's a к.с."

"Yeah, and everybody knows exactly how he got it. We would need a goy."

Takifman brooded over the magazine, pinching his lips. Finally, he said: "A Jew is never poor."

"Oh, here he comes. Takifman, the fanatic. Okay, we've got the Torah. You try it for collateral at the Bank of Canada."

"For shame," Takifman said, appalled.

"Listen here, *Time* is a magazine of current affairs. The Torah is an old story. They are discussing here economics."

"The Torah is nothing to laugh."

"But you are, Takifman."

"A Jew is never poor," Takifman insisted. "Broke?" Sometimes. Going through hard times? Maybe. In a strange country? Always. But poor, never."

Tansky threw his dishrag on the counter. "We are the same as everybody else," he shouted.

"What the hell!"

"Now listen, you listen here, with Chief Rabbi Takifman I don't agree, but the same — "

"You know what, Tansky. You can stuff that where the monkey put his fingers."

Sugarman finished reading the article. "What are you all so excited about?" he asked. "Can't you see this magazine is full of advertisements?"

Everybody turned to look at him.

"According to my son, and he ought to know, these magazines are all under the heel of the big advertisers. They say whatever the advertisers want."

"So you mean it's the advertisers who say we're poor and dirty?"

"You win the sixty-four dollars."

"*Why*, smart-guy?"

"Why? Did I say I know everything? All I said was that according to my son it is the advertisers who – "

"Jews and artists are never poor," Takifman persisted. "How could they be?"

"We are the same as everybody else," Tansky shouted. "Idiots!"

"A Jew is never poor. It would be impossible."

The Summer My
Grandmother was Supposed
to Die

The Summer My Grandmother was Supposed to Die

Dr. Katzman discovered the gangrene on one of his monthly visits. "She won't last a month," he said.

He said the same the second month, the third and the fourth, and now she lay dying in the heat of the back bedroom.

"God in heaven," my mother said, "what's she holding on for?"

The summer my grandmother was supposed to die we did not chip in with the Greenbaums to take a cottage in the Laurentians. My grandmother, already bed-ridden for seven years, could not be moved again. The doctor came twice a week. The only thing was to stay in the city and wait for her to die or, as my mother said, pass away. It was a hot summer, her bedroom was just behind the kitchen, and when we sat down to eat we could smell her. The dressings on my grandmother's left leg had to be changed several times a day and, according to Dr. Katzman, any day might be her last in this world. "It's in the hands of the Almighty," he said.

"It won't be long now," my father said, "and she'll be better off, if you know what I mean?"

A nurse came every day from the Royal Victorian Order. She arrived punctually at noon and at five to twelve I'd join the rest of the boys under the outside staircase to peek up her dress as she climbed to our second-storey flat. Miss Bailey favoured absolutely beguiling pink panties, edged with lace, and that was better than waiting under the stairs for Cousin Bessie, for instance, who wore enormous cotton bloomers, rain or shine.

I was sent out to play as often as possible, because my mother felt it was not good for me to see somebody dying. Usually, I would just roam the scorched streets. There was Duddy, Gas sometimes, Hershey, Stan, Arty and me.

"Before your grandmaw kicks off," Duddy said, "she's going to roll her eyes and gurgle. That's what they call the death-rattle."

"Aw, you know everything. *Putz*."

"I read it, you jerk," Duddy said, whacking me one, "in Perry Mason."

Home again I would usually find my mother sour and spent. Sometimes she wept.

"She's dying by inches," she said to my father one stifling night, "and none of them ever come to see her. Oh, such children," she added, going on to curse them vehemently in Yiddish.

"They're not behaving right. It's certainly not according to Hoyle," my father said.

Dr. Katzman continued to be astonished. "It must be will-power alone that keeps her going," he said. "That, and your excellent care."

"It's not my mother any more in the back room, Doctor. It's an animal. I want her to die."

"Hush. You don't mean it. You're tired." Dr. Katzman dug into his black bag and produced pills for her to take. "Your wife's a remarkable woman," he told my father.

"You don't so say," my father replied, embarrassed.

"A born nurse."

My sister and I used to lie awake talking about our grandmother. "After she dies," I said, "her hair will go on growing for another twenty-four hours."

"Says who?"

"Duddy Kravitz. Do you think Uncle Lou will come from New York for the funeral?"

"I suppose so."

"Boy, that means another fiver for me. Even more for you."

"You shouldn't say things like that or her ghost will come back to haunt you."

"Well, I'll be able to go to her funeral anyway. I'm not too young any more."

I was only six years old when my grandfather died, and so I wasn't allowed to go to his funeral.

I have one imperishable memory of my grandfather. Once he called me into his study, set me down on his lap, and made a drawing of a horse for me. On the horse he drew a rider. While I watched and giggled he gave the rider a beard and the fur-trimmed round hat of a rabbi, a *straimel*, just like he wore.

My grandfather had been a Zaddik, one of the Righteous, and I've been assured that to study Talmud with him had been an illuminating experience. I wasn't allowed to go to his funeral, but years later I was shown the telegrams of condolence that had come from Eire and Poland and even Japan. My grandfather had written many books: a translation of the Book of Splendour (the Zohar) into modern Hebrew, some twenty years work, and lots of slender volumes of sermons, hasidic tales, and rabbinical commentaries. His books had been published in Warsaw and later in New York.

"At the funeral," my mother said, "they had to have six motorcycle policemen to control the crowds. It was such a heat that twelve women fainted – and I'm *not* counting Mrs. Waxman from upstairs. With her, you know, *anything* to fall into a man's arms. Even Pinsky's. And did I tell you that there was even a French Canadian priest there?"

"Aw, you're kidding me."

"The priest was some *knacker*. A bishop maybe. He used to study with the *zeyda*. The *zeyda* was a real personality, you know. Spiritual and worldly-wise at the same time. Such personalities they don't make any more. Today rabbis and peanuts come in the same size."

But, according to my father, the *zeyda* (his father-in-law) hadn't been as celebrated as all that. "There are things I could say," he told me. "There was another side to him."

My grandfather had sprung from generations and generations of rabbis, his youngest son was a rabbi, but none of his grandchildren would be one. My Cousin Jerry was already a militant socialist. I once heard him say, "When the men at the kosher bakeries went out on strike the *zeyda* spoke up against them on the streets and in the *shuls*. It was of no consequence to him that the men were grossly underpaid. His superstitious followers had to have bread. Grandpappy," Jerry said, "was a prize reactionary."

A week after my grandfather died my grandmother suffered a stroke. Her right side was completely paralysed. She couldn't speak. At first it's true, she could manage a coherent word or two and move her right hand enough to write her name in Hebrew. Her name was Malka. But her condition soon began to deteriorate.

My grandmother had six children and seven step-children, for my grandfather had been married before. His first

wife had died in the old country. Two years later he had
married my grandmother, the only daughter of the most
affluent man in the *shtetl,* and their marriage had been a
singularly happy one. My grandmother had been a beautiful
girl. She had also been a shrewd, resourceful, and patient
wife. Qualities, I fear, indispensible to life with a Zaddik.
For the synagogue paid my grandfather no stipulated salary
and much of the money he picked up here and there he
had habitually distributed among rabbinical students, needy
immigrants and widows. A vice, for such it was to his impecunious family, which made him as unreliable a provider
as a drinker. To carry the analogy further, my grandmother
had to make hurried, surreptitious trips to the pawnbroker
with her jewellery. Not all of it to be redeemed, either. But
her children had been looked after. The youngest, her
favourite, was a rabbi in Boston, the oldest was the actor-
manager of a Yiddish theatre in New York, and another
was a lawyer. One daughter lived in Montreal, two in
Toronto. My mother was the youngest daughter and when
my grandmother had her stroke there was a family conclave
and it was decided that my mother would take care of her.
This was my father's fault. All the other husbands spoke
up – they protested hotly that their wives had too much
work – they could never manage it – but my father detested
quarrels and so he was silent. And my grandmother came
to stay with us.

Her bedroom, the back bedroom, had actually been
promised to me for my seventh birthday, but now I had to
go on sharing a room with my sister. So naturally I was
resentful when each morning before I left for school my
mother insisted that I go in and kiss my grandmother good-
bye.

"Bouyo-bouyo," was the only sound my grandmother
could make.

During those first hopeful months – "Twenty years ago

who would have thought there'd be a cure for diabetes?"
my father asked. "Where there's life, you know." – my grandmother would smile and try to speak, her eyes charged with
effort; and I wondered if she knew that I was waiting for
her room.

Even later there were times when she pressed my hand
urgently to her bosom with her surprisingly strong left arm.
But as her illness dragged on and on she became a condition
in the house, something beyond hope or reproach, like the
leaky ice-box, there was less recognition and more ritual in
those kisses. I came to dread her room. A clutter of sticky
medicine bottles and the cracked toilet chair beside the
bed; glazed but imploring eyes and a feeble smile, the wet
smack of her crooked lips against my cheeks. I flinched from
her touch. And after two years, I protested to my mother,
"What's the use of telling her I'm going here or I'm going
there? She doesn't even recognize me any more."

"Don't be fresh. She's your grandmother."

My uncle who was in the theatre in New York sent
money regularly to help support my grandmother and, for
the first few months, so did the other children. But once
the initial and sustaining excitement had passed the children
seldom came to our house any more. Anxious weekly visits
– "And how is she today, poor lamb?" – quickly dwindled to
a dutiful monthly looking in, then a semi-annual visit, and
these always on the way to somewhere.

When the children did come my mother was severe with
them. "I have to lift her on that chair three times a day
maybe. And what makes you think I always catch her in
time? Sometimes I have to change her linen twice a day.
That's a job I'd like to see your wife do," she said to my
uncle, the rabbi.

"We could send her to the Old People's Home."

"Now there's an idea," my father said.

"Not so long as I'm alive." My mother shot my father a
scalding look, "Say something, Sam."

"Quarreling will get us nowhere. It only creates bad feelings."

Meanwhile, Dr. Katzman came once a month. "It's astonishing," he would say each time. "She's as strong as a horse."

"Some life for a person," my father said. "She can't speak – she doesn't recognize anybody – what is there for her?"

The doctor was a cultivated man; he spoke often for women's clubs, sometimes on Yiddish literature and other times, his rubicund face hot with menace, the voice taking on a doomsday tone, on the cancer threat. "Who are we to judge?" he asked.

Every evening, during the first few months of my grandmother's illness, my mother would read her a story by Sholem Aleichem. "Tonight she smiled," my mother would report defiantly. "She understood. I can tell."

Bright afternoons my mother would lift the old lady into a wheelchair and put her out in the sun and once a week she gave her a manicure. Somebody always had to stay in the house in case my grandmother called. Often, during the night, she would begin to wail unaccountably and my mother would get up and rock her mother in her arms for hours. But in the fourth year of my grandmother's illness the strain began to tell. Besides looking after my grandmother, my mother had to keep house for a husband and two children. She became scornful of my father and began to find fault with my sister and me. My father started to spend his evenings playing pinochle at Tansky's Cigar & Soda. Weekends he took me to visit his brothers and sisters. Wherever my father went people had little snippets of advice for him.

"Sam, you might as well be a bachelor. One of the other children should take the old lady for a while. You're just going to have to put your foot down for once."

"Yeah, in your face maybe."

My Cousin Libby, who was at McGill, said, "This could

have a very damaging effect on the development of your children. These are their formative years, Uncle Samuel, and the omnipresence of death in the house . . ."

"What you need is a boy friend," my father said. "*And how.*"

After supper my mother took to falling asleep in her chair, even in the middle of Lux Radio Theatre. One minute she would be sewing a patch in my breeches or making a list of girls to call for a bingo party, proceeds for the Talmud Torah, and the next she would be snoring. Then, inevitably, there came the morning she just couldn't get out of bed and Dr. Katzman had to come round a week before his regular visit. "Well, well, this won't do, will it?"

Dr. Katzman led my father into the kitchen. "Your wife's got a gallstone condition," he said.

My grandmother's children met again, this time without my mother, and decided to put the old lady in the Jewish Old People's Home on Esplanade Street. While my mother slept an ambulance came to take my grandmother away.

"It's for the best," Dr. Katzman said, but my father was in the back room when my grandmother held on tenaciously to the bedpost, not wanting to be moved by the two men in white.

"Easy does it, granny," the younger man said.

Aferwards my father did not go in to see my mother. He went out for a walk.

When my mother got out of bed two weeks later her cheeks had regained their normal pinkish hue; for the first time in months, she actually joked with me. She became increasingly curious about how I was doing in school and whether or not I shined my shoes regularly. She began to cook special dishes for my father again and resumed old friendships with the girls on the parochial school board. Not only did my father's temper improve, but he stopped going to Tansky's every night and began to come home early from work. But my grandmother's name was seldom mentioned. Until one evening, after I'd had a fight with my sister, I said, "Why can't I move into the back bedroom now?"

My father glared at me. "Big-mouth."

"It's empty, isn't it?"

The next afternoon my mother put on her best dress and coat and new spring hat.

"Don't go looking for trouble," my father said.

"It's been a month. Maybe they're not treating her right."

"They're experts."

"Did you think I was never going to visit her? I'm not inhuman, you know."

"Alright, go." But after she had gone my father stood by the window and said, "I was born lucky, and that's it."

I sat on the outside stoop watching the cars go by. My father waited on the balcony above, cracking peanuts. It was six o'clock, maybe later, when the ambulance slowed down and rocked to a stop right in front of our house. "I knew it," my father said. "I was born with all the luck."

My mother got out first, her eyes red and swollen, and hurried upstairs to make my grandmother's bed.

"You'll get sick again," my father said.

"I'm sorry, Sam, but what could I do? From the moment she saw me she cried and cried. It was terrible."

"They're recognized experts there. They know how to take care of her better than you do."

"Experts? Expert murderers you mean. She's got bed-sores, Sam. Those dirty little Irish nurses they don't change her linen often enough they hate her. She must have lost twenty pounds in there."

"Another month and you'll be flat on your back again. I'll write you a guarantee, if you want."

My father became a regular at Tansky's again and, once more, I had to go in and kiss my grandmother in the morning. Amazingly, she had begun to look like a man. Little hairs had sprouted on her chin, she had grown a spiky grey moustache, and she was practically bald.

Yet again my uncles and aunts sent five dollar bills, though erratically, to help pay for my grandmother's support. Elderly people, former followers of my grandfather, came to inquire about the old lady's health. They sat in the back bedroom with her, leaning on their canes, talking to themselves and rocking to and fro. "The Holy Shakers," my father called them. I avoided the seamed, shrunken old men because they always wanted to pinch my cheeks or trick me with a dash of snuff and laugh when I sneezed. When the visit with my grandmother was over the old people would unfailingly sit in the kitchen with my mother for another hour, watching her make *lokshen*, slurping lemon tea out of a saucer. They would recall the sayings and books and charitable deeds of the late Zaddik.

"At the funeral," my mother never wearied of telling them, "they had to have six motorcycle policemen to control the crowds."

In the next two years there was no significant change in my grandmother's condition, though fatigue, ill-temper, and even morbidity enveloped my mother again. She fought with her brothers and sisters and once, after a particularly bitter quarrel, I found her sitting with her head in her hands. "If, God forbid, I had a stroke," she said, "would you send me to the Old People's Home?"

"Of course not."

"I hope that never in my life do I have to count on my children for anything."

The seventh summer of my grandmother's illness she was supposed to die and we did not know from day to day when it would happen. I was often sent out to eat at an aunt's or at my other grandmother's house. I was hardly ever at home. In those days they let boys into the left-field bleachers of

Delormier Downs free during the week and Duddy, Gas sometimes, Hershey, Stan, Arty and me spent many an afternoon at the ball park. The Montreal Royals, kingpin of the Dodger farm system, had a marvellous club at the time. There was Jackie Robinson, Roy Campanella, Lou Ortiz, Red Durrett, Honest John Gabbard, and Kermit Kitman. Kitman was our hero. It used to give us a charge to watch that crafty little Jew, one of ours, running around out there with all those tall dumb southern crackers. "Hey, Kitman," we would yell, "Hey, shmo-head, if your father knew you played ball on *shabus* – " Kitman, alas, was all field and no hit. He never made the majors. "There goes Kermit Kitman," we would holler, after he had gone down swinging again, "the first Jewish strike-out king of the International League." This we promptly followed up by bellowing choice imprecations in Yiddish.

It was after one of these games, on a Friday afternoon, that I came home to find a crowd gathered in front of our house.

"That's the grandson," somebody said.

A knot of old people stood staring at our front door from across the street. A taxi pulled up and my aunt hurried out, hiding her face in her hands.

"After so many years," a woman said.

"And probably next year they'll discover a cure. Isn't that always the case?"

The flat was clotted. Uncles and aunts from my father's side of the family, strangers, Dr. Katzman, neighbours, were all milling around and talking in hushed voices. My father was in the kitchen, getting out the apricot brandy. "Your grandmother's dead," he said.

"Where's Maw?"

"In the bedroom with . . . You'd better not go in."

"I want to see her."

My mother wore a black shawl and glared down at a

knot of handkerchief clutched in a fist that had been cracked by washing soda. "Don't come in here," she said.

Several bearded round-shouldered men in shiny black coats surrounded the bed. I couldn't see my grandmother.

"Your grandmother's dead."

"Daddy told me."

"Go wash your face and comb your hair."

"Yes."

"You'll have to get your own supper."

"Sure."

"One minute. The *baba* left some jewellery. The necklace is for Rifka and the ring is for your wife."

"Who's getting married?"

"Better go and wash your face. Remember behind the ears, please."

Telegrams were sent, the obligatory long distance calls were made, and all through the evening relatives and neighbours and old followers of the Zaddik poured into the house. Finally, the man from the funeral parlour arrived.

"There goes the only Jewish businessman in town," Segal said, "who wishes all his customers were German."

"This is no time for jokes."

"Listen, life goes on."

My Cousin Jerry had begun to affect a cigarette holder. "Soon the religious mumbo-jumbo starts," he said to me.

"Wha'?"

"Everybody is going to be sickeningly sentimental."

The next day was the sabbath and so, according to law, my grandmother couldn't be buried until Sunday. She would have to lie on the floor all night. Two grizzly women in white came to move and wash the body and a professional mourner arrived to sit up and pray for her. "I don't trust his face," my mother said. "He'll fall asleep."

"He won't fall asleep."

"You watch him, Sam."

"A fat lot of good prayers will do her now. Alright! Okay! I'll watch him."

My father was in a fury with Segal.

"The way he goes after the apricot brandy you'd think he never saw a bottle in his life before."

Rifka and I were sent to bed, but we couldn't sleep. My aunt was sobbing over the body in the living room; there was the old man praying, coughing and spitting into his handkerchief whenever he woke; and the hushed voices and whimpering from the kitchen, where my father and mother sat. Rifka allowed me a few drags off her cigarette.

"Well, *pisherke*, this is our last night together. Tomorrow you can take over the back room."

"Are you crazy?"

"You always wanted it for yourself, didn't you?"

"She died in there, but."

"So?"

"I couldn't sleep in there now."

"Good night and happy dreams."

"Hey, let's talk some more."

"Did you know," Rifka said, "that when they hang a man the last thing that happens is that he has an orgasm?"

"A wha'?"

"Skip it. I forgot you were still in kindergarten."

"Kiss my Royal Canadian – "

"At the funeral, they're going to open the coffin and throw dirt in her face. It's supposed to be earth from Eretz. They open it and you're going to have to look."

"Says you."

A little while after the lights had been turned out Rifka approached my bed, her head covered with a sheet and her arms raised high. "Bouyo-bouyo. Who's that sleeping in my bed? Woo-woo."

My uncle who was in the theatre and my aunt from Toronto came to the funeral. My uncle, the rabbi, was there too.

"As long as she was alive," my mother said, "he couldn't even send her five dollars a month. I don't want him in the house, Sam. I can't bear the sight of him."

"You're upset," Dr. Katzman said, "and you don't know what you're saying."

"Maybe you'd better give her a sedative," the rabbi said.

"Sam will you speak up for once, please."

Flushed, eyes heated, my father stepped up to the rabbi. "I'll tell you this straight to your face, Israel," he said. "You've gone down in my estimation."

The rabbi smiled a little.

"Year by year," my father continued, his face burning a brighter red, "your stock has gone down with me."

My mother began to weep and she was led unwillingly to a bed. While my father tried his utmost to comfort her, as he muttered consoling things, Dr. Katzman plunged a needle into her arm. "There we are," he said.

I want to sit on the stoop outside with Duddy. My uncle, the rabbi, and Dr. Katzman stepped into the sun to light cigarettes.

"I know exactly how you feel," Dr. Katzman said. "There's been a death in the family and the world seems indifferent to your loss. Your heart is broken and yet it's a splendid summer day . . . a day made for love and laughter . . . and that must seem very cruel to you."

The rabbi nodded; he sighed.

"Actually," Dr. Katzman said, "it's remarkable that she held out for so long."

"Remarkable?" the rabbi said. "It's written that if a man has been married twice he will spend as much time with his first wife in heaven as he did on earth. My father, may he rest in peace, was married to his first wife for seven years and my mother, may she rest in peace, has managed to keep alive for seven years. Today in heaven she will be able to join my father, may he rest in peace."

Dr. Katzman shook his head. "It's amazing," he said. He told my uncle that he was writing a book based on his experiences as a healer. "The mysteries of the human heart."

"Yes."

"Astonishing."

My father hurried outside. "Dr. Katzman, please. It's my wife. Maybe the injection wasn't strong enough. She just doesn't stop crying. It's like a tap. Can you come in, please?"

"Excuse me," Dr. Katzman said to my uncle.

"Of course." My uncle turned to Duddy and me. 'Well, boys," he said, "what would you like to be when you grow up?"

The Red Menace

The Red Menace

"How," Tansky wanted to know, "could he have created the whole lousy world in seven lousy days when even in this modern scientific age it takes longer than that to build one lousy house? Answer me that, big-mouth."

Tansky, a dedicated communist, worked assiduously during elections for the Labour-Progressive candidates, canvasing for Fred Rose, and after his conviction in the Gouzenko case, nailing up posters for Mike Buhay. Buhay who, in his London days, had mixed with Clem Atlee and Morrison.

"You heard what Maurice Hartt has to say about Buhay and your party. The Labour-Progressives, he says, are as much a party as Ex Lax is a chocolate. . . ."

Hartt had also tripped up Buhay in the provincial legislature, asking him why he didn't work for a living.

"Because," Buhay had replied, "I don't want to do anything that would contribute to the capitalist system."

Then why, Hartt retorted, does your wife work?

"Well," Buhay said, "somebody in the family has to earn a living."

The regulars were tolerant of Tansky's communism, but unresponsive.

"If you ask me," Segal said, "*all* politicians are dirty crooks. Promise, promise, promise, that's before elections. All they want to do is line their pockets."

Not all the men were non-voters like Segal. The horse players and a majority of the gin rummy bunch unfailingly voted for the Liberal candidate.

"Aw, it just wouldn't look good for our people to elect a commie again. You know what I mean?"

In our riding, *Time* ventured, the big battle was between Liberals and Communists. "Communist-voting Cartier riding, an anomaly in conservative Quebec, is heavily industrial. About 40 per cent of the voters are French Canadians. Communists make their appeal to the other 60 per cent, which includes Jewish, Ukranian, Hungarian and Polish workers. Cartier also includes Montreal's flophouse, red-light and underworld districts where votes go to the highest bidder."

Well, yes, but . . .

The truth is Lou and some of the others voted Liberal because their sons, impecunious McGill students, were hired each time there was a federal, provincial or civic election, to go down to the cemeteries with notebooks and compile lists of all those who had died since the last census. Other students were paid to represent the dead at the polls, which, naturally enough, enraged Tansky.

"Let's face it," Sugarman said placatingly. "Most of them would have voted Liberal anyway."

"It's a typical corruption of the democratic process. So-called."

"Look at it another way, then. In Russia there's no problem."

Tansky, the first of many communists I've known, was always extremely kind to me. When I came in on a message he slipped me a chocolate biscuit or maybe a piece of bubble gum. Only once did he demand that I commit myself politically.

"Awright," he demanded heatedly, as I entered the store. "Ask the Hersh kid. He can tell us."

"Gwan. What does he know?"

"Listen here," Tansky said, "do you study Canadian history at your lousy school?"

"Sure."

"Tell me what you know about the Riel rebellion?"

"We haven't come to that part yet."

"That doesn't surprise me. Now tell me something else. What does it say in your book? That the Indians were lied to, cheated, and exploited left, right, and center by lousy imperialist adventurers like Jacques Cartier or that the so-called noble explorers saved Canada from the savages?"

"It says that Jacques Cartier was a hero. LaSalle too. It says they were very brave against the Indians."

"You see, at the age of eleven they're already stuffing their heads with capitalist propaganda. I'll bet there's nothing in their lousy book about the fortunes those bringers-of-Christianity made on the fur market."

Although I liked Tansky enormously, there were others, among them my uncles, who were hostile because he defiantly ate pork and remained open for business on Yom Kippur. Our family was orthodox, we disapproved of communists, but there was a certain confusion about who and what actually was red. To begin with, I was led to believe that a communist was somebody who wrung chicken's necks rather than have them slaughtered according to the orthodox ritual. For when I saw Bernie Huberman's mother doing just that to a chicken in her back yard I was given a straight-forward explanation. "She's a communist, a *roite*."

The family downstairs turned out to be communists too
and I was warned not to speak to them. They moved in
around one o'clock one May night while we sat in judg-
ment on the balcony above, eating watermelon. I had been
allowed to stay up late because of the heat wave.

"You see all those little boxes they're moving in," Segal
whispered.

"Yeah," my father responded eagerly.

"You notice how they're all the same size?"

"Yeah?"

"You see how they're all very heavy?"

"Yeah. So?"

"You wait," Segal said, rocking in his chair. "You wait,
Sam."

The next night there was a distinct and persistent rumbl-
ing downstairs and every Wednesday a panel truck came to
pick up small boxes.

"They've got a printing press," my father would brag to
visitors. "An underground newspaper. *Right downstairs from
us.*"

There were no self-confessed communists with me at
parochial school, but once I graduated to Fletcher's Field
High there were plenty of them. Take Danny Feldman, for
instance. Wiry, scornful Danny, who sat only two seats
behind me in Room 41, was a paid-up, card-holding member
of the Young Communist League, and so came in for lots of
heckling from the rest of us. Danny retaliated by ridiculing
our enthusiasm for the achievements of Maurice "Rocket"
Richard, Johnny Greco, and even Jackie Robinson.

"He's a nigger, but. I thought you stuck up for them?"

"The word is Negro. How would you like it if I called you
a kike?"

"Eat shit."

Sports was an idiotic distraction, Danny argued, a trick
to take our minds off the exploitation of our working-class

parents. Whether they were aware of it or not, Buddy O'Connor, Jerry Heffernan, and Pete Morin, the incomparable razzle-dazzle line, were capitalist lackeys.

Danny was adroit at bringing our teachers to the boil too. He wanted to know why our history text books made no mention of Spartacus and neglected to comment on the Allied attempt to overthrow the Russian revolution in 1919.

"You read the wrong books, Feldman," our history teacher said.

"Yeah. Siddown you dirty red."

"Let's chip in and send him to Russia. Waddiya say, guys?"

Danny shouldered his martyrdom with pride. Softly, softly, he infiltrated the F.F.H.S. Cadets Corps and Students' Council. One day Danny was a civilian and the next he was a cadet major, with access to our sub-basement arsenal; and the Students' Council had got up a petition to demand free milk at lunch hours and a ban on the strap. All this came about whilst our interests, as we began to encourage beards and passed from grade nine to ten, shifted from Rocket Richard's scoring ability to Lili St. Cyr's thrilling striptease act at the Gaiety Theatre. Our latest obsession, Miss St. Cyr's unrivaled interpretation of Leda and the Swan, did not satisfy Danny, either. "I've never met such a bunch of decadent jerks in my life," he said.

"Have you seen her, but?"

"Jeez."

"She shaves her pussy."

"It's art, you know. She does it to classical music."

Danny subjected us to a scathing lecture on women's rights. He said the striptease was merely another form of capitalist degradation and, turning on Shubiner, he asked, "How would you like to see your mother strip on stage?"

Which, considering Mrs Shubiner's dimensions, had the rest of us quaking with laughter.

"You're looking for a punch in the nose," Shubiner hissed. "I'm warning you."

Danny and I, it developed, had something in common. Neither of us joined in when they sang *God Save The King* at school assemblies. Danny abhorred all kings and didn't believe in God. I wouldn't sing *God Save The King* because I was opposed to British policy in Palestine. We had something else in common too – or so I hoped. Only the other night Segal, playing gin rummy with my father, had said, "You know those communist youth clubs?"

"Yeah," my father said eagerly.

"You know they have parties every Friday night?"

"Yeah. So?"

"Boy. Oh, boy."

"*What?*"

Segal jerked his White Owl Cigar discreetly in my direction.

"Go and do your homework," my father said.

Now when the rest of the boys in class heckled Danny, I instantly charged to his defense. "Let Danny speak his piece. This is a free country."

"Sez who?"

"Danny never did you any harm."

"I don't like his dumb kisser, okay? It makes me want to puke."

Danny and I walked home from school together and I hinted that I would be interested in meeting some guys – "and dames too," I allowed – who took life more seriously. There were other things besides sports, I said, and I told Danny a dirty Jewish joke, hoping to lead round to the subject of girls again. It was Segal's joke, the one that ended Bloomberg's dead, but I got no further than telling him about this peddler, one of ours, who had a cock as big as a Coorsh's salami, when Danny cut me short.

"You're a chauvinist," he said.

"No kidding? Um, is that bad like?"

"Well, it's not good. Listen, would you be interested in going to a social on Friday night?"

"Don't mind if I do."

That was Tuesday. Wednesday, I hurried to Irving's Barbershop and got a Hollywood haircut. I also allowed myself to be cajoled into a mudpack facial to remove disfiguring blackheads. Thursday, I retrieved my one-button roll sports jacket from the cleaners and bought a hand-painted tie at Morrie Heft's. Friday, I slipped into my new suit trousers and I was ready an hour early. When Danny finally picked me up I was astonished to discover that he was wearing the same smelly old sweater and baggy trousers he came to school in every day.

There was no liquor at the party. They did have a record player, but nobody could boogie. A fuzzy-haired girl with a guitar sat on the floor and led a folk-singing session. *Joe Hill* and *Los Quatro Generales.* When it came my turn to pick a song I slipped my arm around the girl who sat next to me and asked for the one that began,

> If all the girls were like Hedy Lamarr,
> I'd work half as hard and get twice as far.

"Who brought *that* here?" somebody squealed.

"All-You-Eta," I suggested quickly. "How's about that. It's a kind of gag version of *Alouette.* It goes All-you-eta, think of all-you-eta. All – "

"Shettup," Danny pleaded, poking me.

"But that's a clean one."

"It also happens to be," the fuzzy-haired girl said icily, "a tasteless corruption of one of our few authentic French Canadian folk songs."

The Main

The Main

Two streets below our own came the Main. Rich in delights, but also squalid, filthy, and hollering with stores whose wares, whether furniture or fruit, were ugly or damaged. The signs still say FANTASTIC DISCOUNTS or FORCED TO SELL PRICES HERE, but the bargains so bitterly sought after are illusory – and perhaps they always were.

The Main, with something for all our appetites, was dedicated to pinching pennies from the poor, but it was there to entertain, educate and comfort us too. Across the street from the synagogue you could see THE PICTURE THEY CLAIMED COULD NEVER BE MADE. A little further down the street there was the Workman's Circle and, if you liked, a strip show. Peaches, Margo, Lili St. Cyr. Around the corner there was the ritual baths, the *shvitz* or *mikva*, where my grandfather and his cronies went before the High Holidays, emerging boiling red from the highest reaches of the steam rooms to happily flog each other with brushes fashioned of pine tree branches. Where supremely orthodox women went once a month to purify themselves.

It was to the Main, once a year before the High Holidays, that I was taken for a new suit (the itch of the cheap tweed was excruciating) and shoes (with a built-in squeak). We also shopped for fruit on the Main, meat and fish, and here the important thing was to watch the man at the scales. On the Main, too, was the Chinese laundry – "Have you ever seen such hard workers?" – the Italian hat-blocker – "Tony's a good goy, you know. Against Mussolini from the very first." – and strolling French Canadian priests – "Some of them speak Hebrew now." "Well, if you ask me, it's none of their business. Enough's enough, you know." Kids like myself were dragged along on shopping expeditions to carry parcels. Old men gave us snuff, at the delicatessens we were allowed salami butts, card players pushed candies on us for luck, and everywhere we were poked and pinched by the mothers. Absolutely the best that could be said of us was, "He eats well, knock wood," and later, as we went off to school, "He's a rank-one boy."

After the shopping, once our errands had been done, we returned to the Main once more, either for part-time jobs or to study with our *melamud*. Jobs going on the Main included spotting pins in a bowling alley, collecting butcher bills and, best of all, working at a news-stand, where you could devour the *Police Gazette* free and pick up a little extra short-changing strangers during the rush hour. Work was supposed to be good for our character development and the fact that we were paid was incidental. To qualify for a job we were supposed to be "bright, ambitious, and willing to learn". An ad I once saw in a shoe store window read:

PART-TIME BOY WANTED FOR EXPANDING BUSINESS.
EXPERIENCE ABSOLUTELY NECESSARY, BUT NOT ESSENTIAL

Our jobs and lessons finished, we would wander the street in small groups smoking Turret cigarettes and telling jokes.

"Hey, *shmo-hawk*, what's the difference between a mail box and an elephant's ass?"

"I dunno."

"Well, I wouldn't send *you* to mail my letters."

As the French Canadian factory girls passed arm-in-arm we would call out, "I've got the time, if you've got the place."

Shabus it was back to the Main again and the original Young Israel synagogue. While our grandfathers and fathers prayed and gossiped and speculated about the war in Europe in the musty room below, we played chin the bar in the upstairs attic and told jokes that began, "Confucius say. . . ." or, "Once there was an Englishman, an Irishman, and a Hebe . . ."

We would return to the Main once more when we wanted a fight with the pea-soups. Winter, as I recall it, was best for this type of sport. We could throw snowballs packed with ice or frozen horse buns and, with darkness falling early, it was easier to elude pursuers. Soon, however, we developed a technique of battle that served us well even in the spring. Three of us would hide under an outside staircase while the fourth member of our group, a kid named Eddy, would idle provocatively on the sidewalk. Eddy was a good head-and-a-half shorter than the rest of us. (For this, it was rumoured, his mother was to blame. She wouldn't let Eddy have his tonsils removed and that's why he was such a runt. It was not that Eddy's mother feared surgery, but Eddy sang in the choir of a rich synagogue, bringing in some thirty dollars a month, and if his tonsils were removed it was feared that his voice would go too.) Anyway, Eddy would stand out there alone and when the first solitary pea-soup passed he would kick him in the shins. "Your mother fucks," he'd say.

The pea-soup, looking down on little Eddy, would naturally knock him one on the head. Then, and only then, would we emerge from under the staircase.

"Hey, that's my kid brother you just slugged."

And before the bewildered pea-soup could protest, we were scrambling all over him.

These and other fights, however, sprang more out of boredom than from racial hatred, not that there were no racial problems on the Main.

If the Main was a poor man's street, it was also a dividing line. Below, the French Canadians. Above, some distance above, the dreaded WASPS. On the Main itself there were some Italians, Yugoslavs and Ukrainians, but they did not count as true Gentiles. Even the French Canadians, who were our enemies, were not entirely unloved. Like us, they were poor and coarse with large families and spoke English badly.

Looking back, it's easy to see that the real trouble was there was no dialogue between us and the French Canadians, each elbowing the other, striving for WASP acceptance. We fought the French Canadians stereotype for stereotype. If many of them believed that the St. Urbain Street Jews were secretly rich, manipulating the black market, then my typical French Canadian was a moronic gum-chewer. He wore his greasy black hair parted down the middle and also affected an eyebrow moustache. His zoot trousers were belted just under the breastbone and ended in a peg hugging his ankles. He was the dolt who held up your uncle endlessly at the liquor commission while he tried unsuccessfully to add three figures or, if he was employed at the customs office, never knew which form to give you. Furthermore, he only held his liquor commission or customs or any other government job because he was the second cousin of a backwoods notary who had delivered the village vote to the *Union Nationale* for a generation. Other French Canadians were speed cops, and if any of these ever stopped you on the highway you made sure to hand him a folded two dollar bill with your licence.

Wartime shortages, the admirable Protestant spirit of making-do, benefited both Jews and French Canadians. Jews with clean fingernails were allowed to teach within the Protestant School system and French Canadians off the Atwater League and provincial sandlots broke into the International Baseball League. Jean-Pierre Roy won twenty-five games for the Montreal Royals one year and a young man named Stan Breard enjoyed a season as a stylish but no-hit shortstop. Come to think of it, the only French Canadians I heard of were athletes. Of course there was Maurice Richard, the superb hockey player, but there was also Dave Castiloux, a cunning welterweight, and, above all, the wrestler-hero, Yvon Robert, who week after week gave the blond Anglo-Saxon wrestlers what for at the Forum.

Aside from boyhood street fights and what I read on the sports pages, all I knew of French Canadians was that they were clearly hilarious. Our Scots schoolmaster would always raise a laugh in class by reading us the atrocious Uncle Tom-like dialect verse of William Henry Drummond: *Little Baptiste & Co.*

> On wan dark night on Lac St. Pierre,
> De win' she blow, blow, blow,
> An' de crew of de wood scow "Julie Plant"
> Got scar't an' run below –
> Bimeby she blow some more,
> An' de scow bus' up on Lac St. Pierre
> Wan arpent from de shore.

Actually, it was only the WASPS who were truly hated and feared. "Among them," I heard it said, "with those porridge faces, who can tell what they're thinking?" It was, we felt, their country, and given sufficient liquor who knew when they would make trouble?

We were a rude, aggressive bunch round the Main. Cocky too. But bring down the most insignificant, pinched WASP fire insurance inspector and even the most arrogant merchant on the street would dip into the drawer for a ten spot or a bottle and bow and say, "Sir."

After school we used to race down to the Main to play snooker at the Rachel or the Mount Royal. Other days, when we chose to avoid school altogether, we would take the No. 55 streetcar as far as St. Catherine Street, where there was a variety of amusements offered. We could play the pinball machines and watch archaic strip-tease movies for a nickel at the Silver Gameland. At the Midway or the Crystal Palace we could see a double feature and a girlie show for as little as thirty-five cents. The Main, at this juncture, was thick with drifters, panhandlers and whores. Available on both sides of the street were "Tourist Rooms by Day and Night", and everywhere there was the smell of french fried potatoes cooking in stale oil. Tough, unshaven men in checked shirts stood in knots outside the taverns and cheap cafés. There was the promise of violence.

As I recall it, we were always being warned about the Main. Our grandparents and parents had come there by steerage from Rumania or by cattleboat from Poland by way of Liverpool. No sooner had they unpacked their bundles and cardboard suitcases than they were planning a better, brighter life for us, the Canadian-born children. The Main, good enough for them, was not to be for us, and that they told us again and again was what the struggle was for. The Main was for *bummers*, drinkers, and (heaven forbid) failures.

During the years leading up to the war, the ideal of the ghetto, no different from any other in America, was the doctor. This, mistakenly, was taken to be the very apogee of learning and refinement. In those days there also began the familiar and agonizing process of alienation between immigrant parents and Canadian-born children. Our older brothers and cousins, off to university, came home to realize that our parents spoke with embarrassing accents. Even the younger boys, like myself, were going to "their" schools. According to them, the priests had made a tremendous contribution to the exploration and development of this country. Some were heroes. But our parents had other memories, different ideas, about the priesthood. At school we were taught about the glory of the Crusades and at home we were instructed in the bloodier side of the story. Though we wished Lord Tweedsmuir, the Governor-General, a long life each Saturday morning in the synagogue, there were those among us who knew him as John Buchan. From the very beginning there was their history, and ours. Our heroes, and theirs.

Our parents used to apply a special standard to all men and events. "Is it good for the Jews?" By this test they interpreted the policies of Mackenize King and the Stanley Cup play-offs and earthquakes in Japan. To take one example – if the Montreal *Canadiens* won the Stanley Cup it would infuriate the wasps in Toronto, and as long as the English and French were going at each other they left us alone: *ergo*, it was good for the Jews if the *Canadiens* won the Stanley Cup.

We were convinced that we gained from dissension between Canada's two cultures, the English and the French, and we looked neither to England nor France for guidance. We turned to the United States. The real America.

America was Roosevelt, the Yeshiva College, Max Baer, Mickey Katz records, Danny Kaye, a Jew in the Supreme Court, the *Jewish Daily Forward*, Dubinsky, Mrs. Nussbaum of Allen's Alley, and Gregory Peck looking so cute in *Gentleman's Agreement*. Why, in the United States a Jew even wrote speeches for the president. Returning cousins swore they had heard a cop speak Yiddish in Brooklyn. There were the Catskill hotels, Jewish soap operas on the radio and, above all earthly pleasure grounds, Florida.

Miami. No manufacturer had quite made it in Montreal until he was able to spend a month each winter in Miami.

We were governed by Ottawa, we were also British subjects, but our true capital was certainly New York. Success was (and still is) acceptance by the United States. For a boxer this meant a main bout at Madison Square Garden, for a writer or an artist, praise from New York critics, for a businessman, a Miami tan and, today, for comics, an appearance on the Ed Sullivan Show or for actors, not an important part at the Stratford Festival, but Broadway, or the lead in a Hollywood TV series (Lorne Green in *Bonanza*). The outside world, "their" Canada, only concerned us insofar as it affected our living conditions. All the same, we liked to impress the *goyim*. A knock on the knuckles from time to time wouldn't hurt them. So, while we secretly believed that the baseball field or the prize-fighting ring was no place for a Jewish boy, we took enormous pleasure in the accomplishments of, say, Kermit Kitman, the Montreal Royals outfielder, and Maxie Berger, the welterweight.

Streets such as ours and Outremont, where the emergent middle-class and the rich lived, comprised an almost self-contained world. Outside of business there was a minimal contact with the Gentiles. This was hardly petulant clannishness or naive fear. In the years leading up to the war neo-fascist groups were extremely active in Canada. In the United States there was Father Coughlin, Lindberg, and others. We had Adrian Arcand. The upshot was almost the same. So I can recall seeing swastikas and "*A bas les Juifs*" painted on the Laurentian highway. There were suburbs and hotels in the mountains and country clubs where we were not wanted, beaches with signs that read GENTILES ONLY, quotas at the universities, and occasional racial altercations on Park Avenue. The democracy we were being invited to defend was flawed and hostile to us. Without question it was better for us in Canada than in Europe, but this was still their country, not ours.

I was only a boy during the war. I can remember signs in cigar stores that warned us THE WALLS HAVE EARS and THE ENEMY IS EVERYWHERE. I can also recall my parents, uncles and aunts, cracking peanuts on a Friday night and waiting for those two unequalled friends of the Jews, Roosevelt and Walter Winchell, to come off it and get into the war. We admired the British, they were gutsy, but we had more confidence in the United States Marines. Educated by Hollywood, we could see the likes of John Wayne, Gable, and Robert Taylor making minced meat out of the Panzers, while Noel Coward, Laurence Olivier, and others, seen in a spate of British war films, looked all too humanly vulnerable to us. Briefly, then, Pearl Harbour was a day of jubilation, but the war itself made for some confusions. In another country, relatives recalled by my grandparents were being murdered. But on the street in our air cadet uniforms, we F.F.H.S. boys were more interested in seeking out the fabulously wicked V-girls ("They go the limit with guys in uniform, see.") we had read about in the *Herald*. True, we made some sacrifices. American comic books were banned for the duration due, I think, to a shortage of U.S. funds. So we had to put up a quarter on the black market for copies of the *Batman* and *Tip-Top Comics*. But at the same newsstand we bought a page on which four pigs had been printed. When we folded the paper together, as directed, the four pigs' behinds made up Hitler's hateful face. Outside Cooperman's Superior Provisions, where if you were a regular customer you could get sugar without ration coupons, we would chant "Black-market Cooperman! Black-market Cooperman!" until the old man came out, wielding his broom, and sent us flying down the street.

The war in Europe brought about considerable changes within the Jewish community in Montreal. To begin with, there was the coming of the refugees. These men, interned in England as enemy aliens and sent to Canada where they were eventually released, were to make a profound impact on us. I think we had conjured up a picture of the refugees as penurious *hassidim* with packs on their backs. We were eager to be helpful, our gestures were large, but in return we expected more than a little gratitude. As it turned out, the refugees, mostly German and Austrian Jews, were far more sophisticated and better educated than we were. They had not, like our immigrant grandparents, come from *shtetls* in Galicia or Russia. Neither did they despise Europe. On the contrary, they found our culture thin, the city provincial, and the Jews narrow. This bewildered and stung us. But what cut deepest, I suppose, was that the refugees spoke English better than many of us did and, among themselves, had the effrontery to talk in the abhorred German language. Many of them also made it clear that Canada was no more than a frozen place to stop over until a u.s. visa was forthcoming. So for a while we real Canadians were hostile.

For our grandparents who remembered those left behind in Rumania and Poland the war was a time of unspeakable grief. Parents watched their sons grow up too quickly and stood by helplessly as the boys went off to the fighting one by one. They didn't have to go, either, for until the last days of the war Canadians could only be drafted for service within Canada. A boy had to volunteer before he could be sent overseas.

For those of my age the war was something else. I cannot remember it as a black time, and I think it must be so for most boys of my generation. The truth is that for many of us to look back on the war is to recall the first time our fathers earned a good living. Even as the bombs fell and the ships went down, always elsewhere, our country was bursting out of a depression into a period of hitherto unknown prosperity. For my generation the war was hearing of death and sacrifice but seeing with our own eyes the departure from cold-water flats to apartments in Outremont, duplexes and split-levels in the suburbs. It was when we read of the uprising in the Warsaw ghetto and saw, in Montreal, the changeover from poky little *shuls* to big synagogue-cum-parochial schools with stained glass windows and mosaics outside. During the war some of us lost brothers and cousins but in Canada we had never had it so good, and we began the run from rented summer shacks with outhouses in Shawbridge to Colonial-style summer houses of our own and speedboats on the lake in Ste Agathe.

Pinky's Squealer

Pinky's Squealer

One bright, cloudless morning in July 1941, Noah, Gas and Hershey arranged to meet on the balcony of Old Annie's candy store in Prevost, a village in the Laurentians, where their families had taken cottages for the summer. They were determined to climb the mountain behind the Nine Cottages to get to Lac Gandon, where the *goyim* were.

Hershey turned up first.

Old Annie, who was a tiny, grey-haired widow with black, mournful eyes, looked the boy up and down suspiciously. A first-aid kit and a scout knife were strapped to his belt. "What is," she asked, "a revolution?"

Hershey grimaced. "He who hears no evil, speaks no evil."

Old Annie's store was a squat sinking yellow shack all but covered with signs advertising Kik and Sweet Caporal cigarettes. She wasn't called Old Annie because she was sixty-two. Long ago, in Lithuania, the first three children born to her parents had not survived their infancy. So the village miracle-maker had suggested that if another child was born to them they should call her *alte* (old) instantly, and God would understand.

Gas arrived next. He had a BB gun and a package of crumbly egg and onion sandwiches.

"Knock, knock," he said.

"Who's there?" Hershey asked.

"Ago."

"Ago who?"

"Aw, go tell your mother she wants you."

Behind Old Annie's store was the scorched, spiky field that was used as a market. Early every Friday morning the French Canadian farmers arrived with poultry, vegetables and fruit. They were a skeptical bunch, with hard, seamed faces, but the St. Urbain Street wives were more than a match for them and by late afternoon the farmers were drained and grateful to get away. The women, who were ruthless bargainers, spoke a mixture of French, English and Yiddish with the farmers. "So *fiel*, Monsieur, for dis *kleine* chicken? *Vous* crazy?"

Pinky's Squealer saw the two boys sitting on the stoop, waiting for Noah. He approached them diffidently. "Where you goin'?" he asked.

"To China," Gas said.

When the Squealer's mother wanted him to go to the toilet she would step out on her balcony and yell, "Dollink, time to water the teapot." Pinky, who was the Squealer's cousin, was seventeen years old, and his proper name was Milton Fishman. He was rather pious and conducted services at Camp Machia. The Squealer was his informer.

"I've got a quarter," Pinky's Squealer said.

"Grease it well," Gas replied.

Habitually, those families who lived on Clark, St Urbain, Rachel and City Hall clubbed together and took cottages in Prévost for the summer. How they raised the money, what sacrifices they made, were comparatively unimportant – the children required sun. Prévost had an exceedingly small native population and most of the lopsided cottages were owned by French Canadians who lived in Shawbridge, just up the hill. The C.P.R. railway station was in Shawbridge. Prévost, at the foot of the hill, was separated from Shawbridge by that bridge reputedly built by a man named Shaw. It was a crazy-quilt of clapboard shacks and cottages strewn over hills and fields and laced by bumpy dirt roads and an elaborate system of paths. The centre of the village was at the foot of the bridge. Here were Zimmerman's, Blatt's, The Riverside Inn, Stein the butcher, and – on the winding dirt road to the right – the synagogue and the beach. In 1941 Zimmerman and Blatt still ran staunchly competitive general stores on opposite sides of the highway. Both stores were sprawling dumpy buildings badly in need of a paint job and had dance halls and huge balconies – where you could also dance – attached. But Zimmerman had a helper named Zelda and that gave him the edge over Blatt. Zelda's signs were posted all over Zimmerman's.

Over the fruit stall:

AN ORANGE ISN'T A BASEBALL. DON'T HANDLE WHAT YOU
DON'T WANT. THINK OF THE NEXT CUSTOMER.

Over the cash:

IF YOU CAN GET IT CHEAPER BY THAT GANGSTER ACROSS
THE HIGHWAY YOU CAN HAVE IT FOR NOTHING

However, if you could get it cheaper at Blatt's, Zelda always proved that what you had bought was not as fresh or of a cheaper quality.

The beach was a field of spiky grass and tree stumps. Plump, middle-aged ladies, their flesh boiled pink, spread

out blankets and squatted in their bras and bloomers, playing poker, smoking and sipping cokes. The vacationing
cutters and pressers seldom wore bathing suits either. They
didn't swim. They set up card tables and chairs and played
pinochle solemnly, sucking foul cigars and cursing the sun.
The children dashed in and out among them playing tag or
tossing a ball about. Boys staggered between sprawling
sun-bathers, lugging pails packed with ice and shouting:
"Ice-cold drinks. Chawk-lit bahs. Cig'rettes!"

Occasionally, a woman, her wide-brimmed straw hat
flapping as she waddled from table to table, her smile as big
as her aspirations, gold teeth glittering, would intrude on
the card players, asking – nobody's forcing, mind you – if
they would like to buy a raffle in aid of the Mizrachi Fresh
Air Fund or the J.N.F. Naked babies bawled. Plums, peaches,
watermelons were consumed, pits and peels tossed indis-
criminately on the grass. The slow yellow river was unfailingly condemned by the Health Board during the last three
weeks of August, when the polio scare was at its height.
But the children paid no attention. They shrieked with
delight whenever one of their huge mothers descended into
the water briefly to duck herself – once, twice – warn the
children against swimming out too far – then, return, re-
freshed, to her poker game. The French Canadians were too
shocked to complain, but the priests sometimes preached
sermons about the indecency of the Jews. Mort Shub said,
"Liss'n, it's their job. A priest's gotta make a living too."

At night most people crowded into the dancehalls at
Zimmerman's and Blatt's. The kids, like Noah, Gas, and
Hershey, climbed up the windows and, peashooters in their
mouths, took careful aim at the dancers' legs before firing.
Fridays, the wives worked extremely hard cleaning and
cooking for the sabbath. Everybody got dressed up in the
afternoon in anticipation of the arrival of the fathers, who
were met in Shawbridge, most of them having arrived on

the 6.15 excursion train. Then the procession through Shawbridge, down the hill and across the bridge, began; an event
that always horrified the residents of the village. Who were
these outlandish, cigar-chomping men, burdened with watermelons and Kik bottles, salamis and baskets of peaches, yelling at their children, whacking their wives' behinds and –
worst of all – waving merrily at the sombre Scots who sat
petrified on their balconies?

Noah showed up last.

"Pinky's Squealer wants to come with us," Gas said.

"Did you tell him where we're going?"

"Ixnay. You think I'm crazy?"

"He's got a quarter," Hershey said.

Pinky's Squealer showed Noah the quarter.

"All right," Noah said.

Old Annie, shaking her head sadly, watched the four
boys start out across the fields. Noah led. Hershey, who came
next, was Rabbi Druker's son; a scrawny boy with big brown
eyes. His father had a small but devoted following. Hershey
hung around the synagogue every evening and stopped old
men on their way to prayers. "Give me a nickel and I'll give
you a blessing." He didn't do too badly. "I'm holy as hell,"
he told Noah one evening.

Gas, trailing behind, was plump, fair-haired and freckled.

The boys filed down the dirt road that led to the Nine
Cottages, the sun beating against their brown bodies. They
passed Kravitz's cottage, with its smelly outhouse, Becky
Goldberg's place, and the shapeless shack that housed ten
shapeless Cohens.

The tall grass at the foot of the mountain was stiff and
yellow and made you itch. There were also mushy patches
where the bullrushes grew, but they avoided those. The
sheltering trees cooled the boys, but they had a long climb
ahead of them. The soft plump ground they tramped on
was padded with pine cones, needles, and dead leaves.

Sunlight filtered deviously among the birch and maple and fir trees and the mountain had a dark damp smell to it. There was the occasional cawing of crows, they saw two woodpeckers and, once, a humming-bird. They reached the top of the mountain about one o'clock and sat down on an open patch of ground to eat their lunch. Gas chased around after grasshoppers, storing them in an old mayonnaise jar that had two holes punched in the top. After they had finished their sandwiches they started out again, this time down the other side of the mountain. The foliage thickened and in their eagerness to get along quickly, they scratched their legs and arms in the bush, stumbling into the occasional ditch concealed by leaves and bruising their ankles against jagged stones. They heard voices in the distance. Noah, who had been given the BB gun, pulled back the catch. Gas scooped up a rock, Hershey unstrapped his scout knife. "We'll be late for *shabus*," Pinky's Squealer said "Maybe we should go back?"

"Go ahead," Hershey said. "But watch out for snakes, eh?"

"I didn't say anything."

Voices, laughter too now, came splashing through the trees. The ground began to level off and, just ahead, they made out the beach. There were real canoes, a diving-board, and lots of crazy-coloured umbrellas and deck-chairs. The boys approached the beach cautiously, crouching in the bushes. Noah was amazed. The men were tall and slender and the women were awfully pretty, lying out in the sun there, just like that, not afraid of anything. There was no yelling or watermelon peels or women in bloomers. Everything was so clean. Beautiful, almost.

Gas was the first to notice the soft drink stand. He turned to Pinky's Squealer. "You've got the quarter. Go get us Pepsis."

"Gas should go," Hershey said. "He's the least Jewish-looking of the gang. Look at his nose – Christ! They'll take him for a *goy* easy."

"You can have my quarter."

"Aw, go water your tea-kettle," Gas said. "Maybe I don't look as Jewish as you or Noah, but they can always tell by pulling down your pants . . ."

They all giggled.

"It's not so funny," Hershey said. "That's how they found out about my uncle, who was killed in Russia."

"You're all chicken," Noah said. "I'm going. But I'm having my coke right out there on the beach. If you want anything to drink you'll have to come too."

A convertible Ford pulled away and that revealed the sign to them. Gas noticed it first. Suddenly, he pointed. "Hey, look!"

THIS BEACH
IS
RESTRICTED
TO GENTILES

That changed everything. Noah, his excitement mounting, said they would hang around until evening and then, when the beach was deserted, steal the sign.

"Yeah, and walk back in the dark, eh?" Pinky's Squealer said. "It's Friday, you know. Aint *your* paw coming?"

Gas and Hershey looked puzzled. Both of them had been forbidden to play with Noah by their mothers. Pinky's Squealer made sense, but if Noah intended to stay they would look cowardly if they left him behind. Noah certainly wanted to stay. Having his father up for the weekend usually meant two days of quarreling.

"Aw, in a hundred years we'll all be dead," Gas said.

Pinky's Squealer waited, kicking the stump of a tree petulantly. "If you come with me, Hershey, you can have my quarter."

"Watch out for snakes," Hershey said.

Pinky's Squealer ran off.

The afternoon dragged on slowly, but at last the sun lowered and a strong breeze was starting up. Only a few stragglers remained on the beach.

"Is a Gentile a Catholic and a Protestant too?" Hershey asked.

"Yeah," Noah said.

"But they're different," Hershey said, "aren't they?"

"Different," Gas said. "You know the difference between Hitler and Mussolini?"

Noah decided that as it was getting late they would have to risk it, stragglers and all. The few couples who remained were intent on each other and wouldn't notice them if they were cunning. Noah said that he and Gas should stroll out on to the beach, approaching the sign from different directions, nonchalantly. It didn't look as if it was stuck very solidly into the sand. Hershey was to holler if he saw anybody coming for them. He had stones and the BB gun.

So the two boys sauntered innocently out on to the beach. Noah whistled. Gas pretended to be searching for something. The wind kicked up gusts of sand and the sun, sinking still lower, was a blaze in the opposite hills. Suddenly, frantically, the two boys were yanking at the sign. Gas shook with laughter, tears rolling down his cheeks. Noah cursed. They heard, piercing the stillness, a high-pitched shout. "Look out!"

Gas let go, and ran off. Flying for the woods.

"Hurry!"

Noah persisted. A man, waving a canoe paddle, was running toward him. Noah gave one last, frenzied tug, and the sign broke free. The man was about twenty feet away now, wielding his paddle viciously. His eyes were wild. "You little son of a bitch!"

Noah swerved, racing for the bushes. A shower of pebbles bounced off his back. The paddle swooshed through the air behind him. But he was fast. Once in the bushes he scampered off, zigzaging into the mountain. He ran and ran and ran. Finally, clutching the sign in his hands, he tumbled down on the pine needles, his heart hammering.

Noah couldn't find Gas anywhere, but Hershey loomed up from behind a rock. Darkness fell quickly and they soon realized they were lost. Lost, and without a flashlight. Possibly, they were moving in circles. For all they knew they might come out of the woods again at Lac Gandon.

Noah and Hershey had stopped climbing, they had reached a level bit of ground and then all at once they heard many voices. Light beams shot through the darkness. Hastily, the boys concealed the sign under a mess of decaying leaves and climbed up the nearest tree – their pockets filled with stones. The voices and probing lights came nearer.

"Hershey!"

"Noah!"

"Boys!"

"HALLO!"

The boys began to quake with laughter. Every able-bodied man in Prevost must have been out on the mountain that night, armed with pitchforks, rakes, clubs and baseball bats. Noah and Hershey had never thought they'd be grateful to Pinky's Squealer, but they were that Friday night. They slid down the tree and uncovered the sign and that was their night of glory in Prévost. Nothing was too good for them. Sunday morning Noah, Hershey, Mort Shub, and Gas planted the sign on their own beach. When the others came out to swim, they read:

> **THIS BEACH**
> **IS**
> **RESTRICTED**
> **TO ~~GENTILES~~**
> **LITVAKS**

Bambinger

Bambinger

We needed money. But we could not, like the Isenbergs next door, put a "Room To Let" sign in the window. We had standards to maintain.

"Taking in a refugee, a single man," my mother argued, "would help to fight human suffering. It might also mean a husband for Cousin Bessie, poor thing."

So in November, 1942, a phone call was made to the proper agency, and we got our first roomer, a refugee, without advertising. Herr Bambinger was a slight, stooping man with a shiny bald head and almost no chin. He wore thick glasses with steel frames and, even though he rolled his own cigarettes, he used a tortoise-shell cigarette holder.

"I guess," my mother said, "you're thinking of settling down. You'll be looking for a wife."

"You bet your bottom dollar he is," my father said.

On Friday Cousin Bessie was produced at dinner and on Saturday my parents cornered Herr Bambinger.

"Beauty," my mother said, "is only skin deep."

"Ach, so."

"What a man wants in a wife is somebody steady," my father said, offering Herr Bambinger a shot of apricot brandy. "Somebody with a little something in the bank."

Herr Bambinger didn't, like the other refugees, drink black coffee endlessly at the Old Vienna and pontificate about what a dull, uncultured country Canada was. Bambinger spent most of his evenings smoking in the dark in his room, the back bedroom. He wrote a prodigious number of letters, always filling the rice paper pages from top to bottom with the smallest, tightest handwriting I had ever seen. The letters went to the International Red Cross and refugee organizations and camps all over the world, but nothing ever came for him unless it was his own letters returned or copies of the *Aufbau*. Bambinger took a considerable interest in me. He convinced my mother that comic books were a bad influence. Superman, he said, was a glorification of fascism, and the Batman and Robin had a thinly – "very thinly," he said – disguised homosexual relationship. "I don't advise," he'd say to my mother, "that the boy should go without a scarf in such coldness." A couple of days later it was, "The boy shouldn't keep the elbows on the table when he eats." Or, another time, as he switched off the radio abruptly, "A boy can't do his studies and listen to the wireless at the same time."

My parents believed that Herr Bambinger had my welfare at heart and when I protested against his intrusions they disciplined me. One Saturday afternoon my mother forced me to go out for a walk with Herr Bambinger.

"Why should I miss the ball game, but?" I asked.

"The poor man has a wife and child of your age and he doesn't know where they are or if they're still alive."

Bambinger – vengefully, I thought – led me to the art museum on Sherbrooke Street. "It is never too early," he said, lighting a cigarette, "for one to learn appreciation of the arts."

"How's about a cig for me?"

"Nicotine is bad for growing boys."

"If you're too cheap to butt me just say so."

"You are not only stupid. You are very impudent. If you were my boy it would not be so. I'd teach you respect."

"Well, I'm not your boy, see."

When Bambinger and I finally did tangle it was over coffee. Coffee, if you remember, was rationed during the war, and at the age of twelve a boy became entitled to a share. There were coupons for it provided in this book. I had waited impatiently for my twelfth birthday and the day after it I demanded a cup. My mother smiled a little. But Bambinger shot her a warning glance and regarded me reproachfully across the table.

"You know you're not allowed to drink coffee," my mother said. "You're still a child."

My sister grinned and took a long sip from her cup.

"As far as the legally elected government of Canada is concerned I am, as of yesterday, allowed to drink coffee."

"The government is full of anti-semites," my father pronounced compulsively.

But I could see that my mother's resolve was weakening.

"One cup," I pleaded. "Would it break your heart?"

"Your mother's right. Coffee is bad for a growing boy."

Staying up late, according to Bambinger, would also stunt my growth. As did evenings spent at the Park Bowling Academy.

"This is family business, so keep your big nose out of it."

"Apologize to Mr. Bambinger immediately."

"Either I get my legal ration or I destroy my coupons."

"You will do no such thing. Now apologize to Mr. Bambinger."

Bambinger smiled mockingly at me, waiting.

"Well, the hell with you," I shouted, turning on Bambinger. "Why'd you run away from Hitler, you chicken? Couldn't you have stayed behind and fought in the under-

ground? Wouldn't that have been better than running out
on your wife and kid to save your own skin?"

My mother slapped me.

"Okay," I said, bolting. "I'm leaving home."

Outside, it was raining. Fists jammed into my wind-
breaker pockets, hastily packed kitbag bouncing against my
back, I jogged to the Park Bowling Academy, where Hershey
was spotting pins. "Hey," I said, "how'd you like to run away
from home with me?"

Hershey wiped the sweat from his forehead, pondering
my proposition. "Cancha wait until Monday? We're having
latkas for dinner tomorrow."

Walking back to St. Urbain with Hershey, I told him
about my troubles with Bambinger. It began to rain harder
and we sheltered under a winding outside staircase. "Hey,
would you do me a favour?" I asked.

"No."

"*Thanks.*"

"What do you want me to do?"

I asked him to ring my doorbell and tell my mother I
had fainted or something. "Say you found me lying in the
gutter."

"You're chicken. I knew it. You're not running away from
home."

Hershey gave me a shove and I scooped up my kitbag
to slug him. He began to run. It was almost ten-thirty, the
rain had turned to snow.

"You've come back," my mother said, seemingly overjoyed.

"Only for tonight."

"Come," she said, taking me by the hand. "We've just had
the most wonderful news."

Bambinger was actually dancing round the dining room
table with my sister. He wore a paper hat and had let his
glasses slip down to the tip of his nose. "Well," he said, "well,
well, the prodigal returns. I told you not to worry."

Bambinger smiled and pinched my cheek, he pinched it very hard before I managed to break free.

"They were going to send out the police to look for you."

"Mrs. Bambinger and Julius are safe," my mother said, clapping her hands.

"They're coming here from Australia," my father said. "By ship. There was a telegram."

"I'm soaked. I'll be lucky if I didn't catch pneumonia."

"Yeah. Just look at him," my father said. "You'd think he'd been out swimming. And what did he prove? Nothing."

"I'll tell you what," Bambinger said, "you may still be too young for coffee but a little brandy won't hurt you."

Everybody laughed. Thrusting past Bambinger, I fled to the bedroom. My mother followed me inside. "Why are you crying?"

"I'm not crying – I'm soaked."

The dining room vibrated with laughter.

"Go back to your party. Enjoy yourself."

"I want you to apologize to Mr. Bambinger."

I didn't say a word.

"You will be allowed one cup of coffee a week."

"Was that his idea?"

My mother looked at me, astonished.

"Alright. I'm going. I'll apologize to him."

I went to Bambinger's room with him. "Well," he said with an ironical smile, "speak up. I won't bite you."

"My mother says to tell you I'm sorry."

"Ach, so."

"You're always picking on me."

"Am I?"

"Maybe they don't understand. I do, but."

Bambinger rolled a cigarette, deliberately slow, and let me stand there for a while before he said, "Your grammar is atrocious."

"This is my room and my bed."

"Ach, so."

"It shoulda been anyway. I was promised. Only they made me stay with my sister and rented it to you instead."

"I think your parents need the money."

"I apologized. Can I go now?"

"You can go."

The next morning Bambinger and I couldn't look at each other and a week went by without his once admonishing, correcting, or trying to touch me. A thick letter came from Australia and Bambinger showed us photographs of a small unsmiling boy in a foreign-type suit that was obviously too tight for him. His wife had stringy grey hair, a squint, and what appeared to be a gold tooth. Bambinger read passages from his letter aloud to my parents. His family, I learned, would not be arriving in Canada for six weeks, the boat trip alone taking a month.

Bambinger now applied himself entirely to work and frugality. He gave up smoking even hand-rolled cigarettes and put in overtime at the factory whenever it was available. On weekends Bambinger searched for bargains. One day he came home with a suit from a fire-sale for his boy and on another he purchased an ancient washing machine and set to repairing it himself. He picked up a table and chairs at an auction and bought a reconditioned vacuum cleaner at a bazaar. All these, and other articles, he stored in the shed; and all this time he ignored me.

One day I surprised Bambinger with a collection of nearly-new comic books – "For your kid," I said, fleeing – and the next morning I found them on top of the garbage pail in the shed. "Julius will not read such trash," he said.

"They cost me a nickel each, but."

"The thought was nice. But you wasted your money."

On Saturday afternoon, only a week before Mrs. Bambinger and Julius should have arrived, my father came into the kitchen carrying the newspaper. He whispered something to my mother.

"Yes, that's the name of the ship. Oh, my God."

Bambinger staggered in from the shed, supporting a table with three legs.

"Brace yourself," my father said.

Bambinger seized the newspaper and read the story at the bottom of page one.

"You can never tell," my mother said. "They could be in a lifeboat. That happens all the time, you know."

"Where there's life, there's hope."

Bambinger went into his room and stayed there for three days and when he came out again it was only to tell us he was moving. The morning of his departure he summoned me to his room. "You can have your bed back again." he said.

I just stood there.

"You've been deprived of a lot. You've suffered a good deal. Haven't you? *Little bastard.*"

"I didn't sink the ship," I said, frightened.

Bambinger laughed. "Ach, so," he said.

"Why you moving?"

"I'm going to Toronto."

That was a lie. Two weeks later I saw Bambinger walking toward me on St. Catherine Street. He was wearing a new suit, a fedora with a wide brim, and glasses with thick shell frames. The girl with him was taller than he was. At first I intended to ask him if he was ever going to come round for the stuff in the shed but I crossed to the other side of the street before he spotted me.

Benny, the War in Europe, and Myerson's Daughter Bella

Benny, the War in Europe, and Myerson's Daughter Bella

When Benny was sent overseas in the autumn of 1941 his father, Garber, decided that if he had to yield one son to the army it might just as well be Benny, who was a dumbie and wouldn't push where he shouldn't; Mrs. Garber thought, he'll take care, my Benny will watch out; and Benny's brother Abe proclaimed, "When he comes back, I'll have a garage of my own, you bet, and I'll be able to give him a job." Benny wrote every week, and every week the Garbers sent him parcels full of good things a St. Urbain Street boy should always have, like salami and pickled herring and *shtrudel*. The food parcels never varied and the letters – coming from Camp Borden and Aldershot and Normandy and Holland – were always the same too. They began – "I hope you are all well and good" – and ended – "don't worry, all the best to everybody, thank you for the parcel."

When Benny came home from the war in Europe, the Garbers didn't make an inordinate fuss, like the Shapiros

did when their first-born son returned. They met him at the
station, of course, and they had a small dinner for him.

Abe was overjoyed to see Benny again. "Atta boy," was
what he kept saying all evening, "Atta boy, Benny."

"You shouldn't go back to the factory," Mr. Garber said.
"You don't need the old job. You can be a help to your
brother Abe in his garage."

"Yes," Benny said.

"Let him be, let him rest," Mrs. Garber said. "What'll
happen if he doesn't work for two weeks?"

"Hey, when Artie Segal came back," Abe said, "he told
me that in Italy there was nothing that a guy couldn't get for
a couple of Sweet Caps. Was he shooting me the bull or
what?"

Benny had been discharged and sent home not because
the war was over, but because of the shrapnel in his leg.
He didn't limp too badly and he wouldn't talk about his
wound or the war, so at first nobody noticed that he had
changed. Nobody, that is, except Myerson's daughter, Bella.

Myerson was the proprieter of Pop's Cigar & Soda, on St.
Urbain, and any day of the week you could find him there
seated on a worn, peeling kitchen chair playing poker with
the men of the neighbourhood. He had a glass eye and
when a player hesitated on a bet, he would take it out and
polish it, a gesture that never failed to intimidate. His
daughter, Bella, worked behind the counter. She had a club-
foot and mousey brown hair and some more hair on her face,
and although she was only twenty-six, it was generally agreed
that she would end up an old maid. Anyway she was the
one – the first one – to notice that Benny had changed. The
very first time he appeared in Pop's Cigar & Soda after his
homecoming, she said to him, "What's wrong, Benny?"

"I'm all right," he said.

Benny was short and skinny with a long narrow face, a
pulpy mouth that was somewhat crooked, and soft black

eyes. He had big, conspicuous hands which he preferred to keep out of sight in his pockets. In fact he seemed to want to keep out of sight altogether and whenever possible, he stood behind a chair or in a dim light so that the others wouldn't notice him. When he had failed the ninth grade at F.F.H.S, Benny's class master, a Mr. Perkins, had sent him home with a note saying: "Benjamin is not a student, but he has all the makings of a good citizen. He is honest and attentive in class and a hard worker. I recommend that he learn a trade."

When Mr. Garber had read what his son's teacher had written, he had shaken his head and crumpled up the bit of paper and said – "A trade?" – he had looked at his boy and shaken his head and said – "A trade?"

Mrs. Garber had said stoutly, "Haven't you got a trade?"

"Shapiro's boy will be a doctor," Mr. Garber had said.

"Shapiro's boy," Mrs. Garber had said.

Afterwards, Benny had retrieved the note and smoothed out the creases and put it in his pocket, where it had remained.

The day after his return to Montreal, Benny showed up at Abe's garage having decided that he didn't want two weeks off. That pleased Abe a lot. "I can see that you've matured since you've been away," Abe said. "That's good. That counts for you in this world."

Abe worked extremely hard, he worked night and day, and he believed that having Benny with him would give his business an added kick. "That's my kid brother Benny," Abe used to tell the taxi drivers. "Four years in the infantry, two of them up front. A tough *hombre*, let me tell you."

For the first few weeks Abe was pleased with Benny. "He's slow," he reported to their father, "no genius of a mechanic, but the customers like him and he'll learn." Then Abe began to notice things. When business was slow, Benny, instead of taking advantage of the lull to clean up the shop, used to sit shivering in a dim corner, with his hands folded tight on his lap. The first time Abe noticed his brother behaving like that, he said, "What's wrong? You got a chill?"

"No. I'm all right."

"You want to go home or something?"

"No."

Whenever it rained, and it rained often that spring, Benny was not to be found around the garage, and that put Abe in a foul temper. Until one day during a thunder shower, Abe tried the toilet door and discovered that it was locked. "Benny," he yelled, "you come out, I know you're in there."

Benny didn't answer, so Abe fetched the key. He found Benny huddled in a corner with his head buried in his knees, trembling, with sweat running down his face in spite of the cold.

"It's raining," Benny said.

"Benny, get up. What's wrong?"

"Go away. It's raining."

"I'll get a doctor, Benny."

"No. Go away. Please, Abe."

"But Benny . . ."

Benny began to shake violently, just as if an inner whip had been cracked. Then, after it had passed, he looked up at Abe dumbly, his mouth hanging open. "It's raining," he said.

The next morning Abe went to see Mr. Garber. "I don't know what to do with him," he said.

"The war left him with a bad taste," Mrs. Garber said.

"Other boys went to the war," Abe said.

"Shapiro's boy," Mr. Garber said, "was an officer."

"Shapiro's boy," Mrs. Garber said. 'You give him a vacation, Abe. You insist. He's a good boy. From the best."

Benny didn't know what to do with his vacation, so he slept in late, and began to hang around Pop's Cigar & Soda.

"I don't like it, Bella," Myerson said, "I need him here like I need a cancer."

"Something's wrong with him psychologically," one of the card players ventured.

But obviously Bella enjoyed having Benny around and after a while Myerson stopped complaining. "Maybe the boy is serious," he confessed, "and with her club foot and all that stuff on her face, I can't start picking and choosing. Besides, it's not as if he was a crook. Like Huberman's boy."

"You take that back. Huberman's boy was a victim of circumstances. He was taking care of the suitcase for a stranger, a complete stranger, when the cops had to mix in."

Bella and Benny did not talk much when they were together. She used to knit, he used to smoke. He would watch silently as she limped about the store, silently, with longing, and consternation. The letter from Mr. Perkins was in his pocket. Occasionally, Bella would look up from her knitting. "You feel like a cup coffee?"

"I wouldn't say no."

Around five in the afternoon he would get up, Bella would come round the counter to give him a stack of magazines to take home, and at night he would read them all from cover to cover and the next morning bring them back as clean as new. Then he would sit with her in the store again, looking down at the floor or at his hands.

One day instead of going home around five in the afternoon, Benny went upstairs with Bella. Myerson, who was watching, smiled. He turned to Shub and said: "If I had a boy of my own, I couldn't wish for a better one than Benny."

"Look who's counting chickens," Shub replied.

Benny's vacation dragged on for several weeks and every morning he sat down at the counter in Pop's Cigar & Soda and every evening he went upstairs with Bella, pretending not to hear the wise-cracks made by the card players as they passed. Until one afternoon Bella summoned Myerson upstairs in the middle of a deal. "We have decided to get married," she said.

"In that case," Myerson said, "you have my permission."

"Aren't you even going to say luck or something?" Bella asked.

"It's your life," Myerson said.

They had a very simple wedding without speeches in a small synagogue and after the ceremony was over Abe whacked his younger brother on the back and said, "Atta boy, Benny. Atta boy."

"Can I come back to work?"

"Sure you can. You're the old Benny again. I can see that."

But his father, Benny noticed, was not too pleased with the match. Each time one of Garber's cronies congratulated him, he shrugged his shoulders and said, "Shapiro's boy married into the Segals."

"Shapiro's boy," Mrs. Garber said.

Benny went back to the garage, but this time he settled down to work hard and that pleased Abe enormously. "That's my kid brother Benny," Abe took to telling the taxi drivers, "married six weeks and he's already got one in the oven. A quick worker, I'll tell you."

Benny not only settled down to work hard, but he even laughed a little, and, with Bella's help, began to plan for the future. But every now and then, usually when there was a slack period at the garage, Benny would shut up tight and sit in a chair in a dark corner. He had only been back at work for three, maybe four, months when Bella went to speak to Abe. She returned to their flat on St. Urbain her face flushed and triumphant. "I've got news for you," she said to Benny. "Abe is going to open another garage on Mount Royal and you're going to manage it."

"But I don't want to, I wouldn't know how."

"We're going to be partners in the new garage."

"I'd rather stay with Abe."

Bella explained that they had to plan for their child's future. Their son, she swore, would not be brought up over a cigar & soda, without so much as a shower in the flat. She wanted a fridge. If they saved, they could afford a car. Next year, she said, after the baby was born, she hoped there would be sufficient money saved so that she could go to a clinic in the United States to have an operation on her foot. "I was to Dr. Shapiro yesterday and he assured me there is a clinic in Boston where they perform miracles daily."

"He examined you?" Benny asked.

"He was very, very nice. Not a snob, if you know what I mean."

"Did he remember that he was at school with me?"

"No," Bella said.

Bella woke at three in the morning to find Benny huddled on the floor in a dark corner with his head buried in his knees, trembling. "It's raining," he said. "There's thunder."

"A man who fought in the war can't be scared of a little rain."

"Oh, Bella. Bella, Bella."

She attempted to stroke his head but he drew sharply away from her.

"Should I send for a doctor?"

"Shapiro's boy maybe?" he asked, giggling.

"Why not?"

"Bella," he said. "Bella, Bella."

"I'm going next door to the Idelsohns to phone for the doctor. Don't move. Relax."

But when she returned to the bedroom he had gone.

Myerson came round at eight in the morning. Mr. and Mrs. Garber were with him.

"Is he dead?" Bella asked.

"Shapiro's boy, the doctor, said it was quick."

"Shapiro's boy," Mrs. Garber said.

"It wasn't the driver's fault," Myerson said.

"I know," Bella said.

Making It with the Chicks

Making It with the Chicks

I wasn't quite eight years old when I first got into trouble over a girl. Her name was Charna, she lived upstairs from me, and we had played together without incident for years. Then, one spring afternoon, it seemed to me that I'd had enough of marbles and one-two-three-RED LIGHT!

"I've got it. We're going to play hospital. I'm the doctor, see, and you're the patient. Is anybody home at your place?"

"No. Why?"

"It's more of an indoors game, like. Come on."

I had only begun my preliminary examination when Charna's mother came home. My punishment was twofold. I had to go to bed without my supper and my mouth was washed out with soup. "You'd better speak to him," my mother said. "It's a lot worse when they pick up that kind of knowledge on the streets."

"It looks like he's very well-informed already," my father said.

If I wasn't, it was clearly my mother's fault. Some years earlier she had assured me that babies came from Eaton's, and whenever she wanted to terrify me into better behaviour she would pick up the phone and say, "I'm going to call Eaton's right this minute and have you exchanged for a girl."

My sister would compulsively add to my discomfort. "Maybe Eaton's won't take him back. This isn't bargain basement week, you know."

"I'll send him to Morgan's, then."

"Morgan's," my father would say, looking up from his evening paper, "doesn't hire Jews."

Duddy Kravitz cured me of the department store myth. He was very knowing about how to make babies. "You do it with a seed. You plant it, see."

"Where, but?"

"*Where*? Jesus H. Christ!"

Duddy was also a shrewd one for making it with the girls. When we were both twelve, just starting to go out on dates, he asked me, "When you go to a social, what do you do first?"

"Ask the prettiest girl for a dance."

"Prick."

Duddy explained that everybody went to the dance with the same notion. The thing to do, he said, was to make a big play for the *third* prettiest girl while all the others were hovering around number one. To further my education, he sold me a copy of *The Art Of Kissing* for a dollar. "When you're through with it," he said, "and if it's still in good condition, you bring it back, and for another fifty cents I'll lend you a copy of *How To Make Love*. Okay?"

The first chapter I turned to in *The Art Of Kissing* was called HOW TO APPROACH A GIRL.

In kissing a girl whose experience with osculation is limited, it is a good thing to work up to the kissing of the lips. Only an arrant fool seizes hold of such a girl, when they are comfortably seated on the sofa, and suddenly shoves his face into her's and smacks her lips. Naturally, the first thing he should do is arrange it so that the girl is seated against the arm of the sofa while he is seated at her side. In this way, she cannot edge away from him when he becomes serious in his attentions.

"Hey," my sister yelled, "how long are you going to be in there?"
"Hay is for horses."
"I've got to take a bath. I'm late."

If she flinches, don't worry. If she flinches and makes an outcry, don't worry. If she flinches, makes an outcry and tries to get up from the sofa, don't worry. Hold her, gently but firmly, and allay her fears with reassuring words.

"When you come out of there I'm going to break your neck."
"You, and what army?"

. . . then your next step is to flatter her in some way. All women like to be flattered. They like to be told they are beautiful even when the mirror throws the lie right back in their ugly faces.
Flatter her!
Ahead of you lies that which had been promised in your dreams, the tender, luscious lips of the girl you love. But don't sit idly by and watch her lips quiver.
Act!

"Why did you stuff the keyhole?"
"Because I've heard of snoopers like you before."

"Oh, *now* I get it. Now I know what you're doing in there. Why you filthy little thing, you'll stop growing."

. . . there has been raised quite a fuss in regard to whether one should close one's eyes while kissing or while being kissed. Personally, I disagree with those who advise closed eyes. To me, there is an additional thrill in seeing, before my eyes, the drama of bliss and pleasure as it is played on the face of my beloved.

"Awright," I said, opening the door, it's all your'n."

Our parties were usually held at a girl's house and it was the done thing to bring along the latest hit parade record. Favourites at the time were *Besame Mucho, Dance Ballerina, Dance,* and *Tico-Tico.* We would boogie for a while and gradually insist on more and more slow numbers, fox trots, until Duddy would leap up, clear his throat, and say, "Hey, isn't the light in here hurting your eyes?"

Next, another boy would try a joke for size.

"Hear what happened to Barbara Stanwyck? Robert Taylor."

"Wha?"

"Robert Tayl'der, you jerk."

"Yeah, and what about Helena Rubinstein?"

"So?"

"Max Factor."

But with the coming of the party-going stage complications set in for me, anyway. Suddenly, my face was encrusted with pimples. I was also small and puny for my age. And, according to the author of *The Art Of Kissing,* it was essential for the man to be taller than the woman.

He must be able to sweep her into his strong arms, and tower over her, and look down into her eyes, and cup her chin in his fingers and then, bend over her face and plant his eager, virile lips on her moist, slightly parted, inviting ones. And, all of these are impossible when the woman is taller than he is. For when the situation is reversed the kiss becomes a ludicrous banality, the physical mastery is gone, everything is gone, but the fact that two lips are touching two other lips. Nothing can be more disappointing.

I had difficulty getting a second date with the same girl and usually the boys had to provide for me. Duddy would get on the phone, hustling some unsuspecting girl, saying, "There's this friend of mine in from Detroit. Would you like to go to a dance with him on Saturday night?"

Grudgingly, the girl would acquiesce, but afterwards she would complain "Why didn't you tell me he was such a runt?"

So Duddy took me aside. "Why don't you try body-building or something?"

I wrote to Joe Weider, the Trainer of Champions, and he promptly sent me a magazine called *How To Build a* STRONG MUSCULAR BODY *with* WEIDER *as Your Leader*.

"Be MASCULINE!
Be DESIRED!
Look in the mirror — ARE YOU
really attractive to LOVE?
What does the mirror reveal? A sickly, pimply string-bean of a fellow — OR — a VIBRANT, masculine looking, romance attracting WEIDER MAN? If YOU were a vivacious, lovely, young woman, which would YOU choose? the tired, listless, drab chap, or the strong, energetic, forceful MAN — able to protect his sweetheart and give her the best things in life?"

Alas, I couldn't afford the price of making Weider my leader. I tried boxing at the "Y" instead and was knocked out my second time in the gym ring. I would have persevered, however, if not for the fact that my usual sparring partner, one Herkey Samuels, had a nasty trick of blowing his nose on his glove immediately before he punched me. Besides, I wasn't getting any taller. I wasn't exactly stunted, but a number of the other boys had already begun to shave. The girls had started to use lipstick and high heels, not to mention brassieres.

Arty, Stan, Hershey, Gas, and I were drifting through high school at the time, and there we got a jolt. All at once the neighbourhood girls, whom we had been pursuing loyally for years, dropped us for older boys. Boys with jobs, McGill boys – anybody – so long as he was eighteen and had the use of a car.

"They think it's such a big deal," Arty said, "because suddenly they've begun to sprout tits."

"Did you see the guy who came to pick up Helen? The world's number one *shmock*."

"What about Libby's date?"

Disconsolate, we would squat on the outside steps on Saturday nights and watch the girls come tripping out in their party dresses, always to settle into a stranger's car, and swim off into the night without even a wave for us. Obviously, a double-feature at the Rialto, a toasted tomato sandwich and a coke afterwards, no longer constituted a bona fide date. That, one of the girls scathingly allowed, was okay "for children" like us, but nowadays they went to fraternity dances or nightclubs and, to hear them tell it, sipped Singapore Slings endlessly.

"Let them have their lousy little fling," Arty advised. "Soon they'll come back crawling for a date. You wait."

We waited and waited until, disheartened, we shunned girls altogether for a period. Instead, we took to playing blackjack on Saturday nights.

"Boy, when I think of all the *mezuma* I blew on Gitel."

"Skip it. I'd rather lose money to a friend, a real friend," Duddy said, scooping up another pot, "than spend it on a girl any time."

"They're getting lousy reps, those whores, running around with strange guys in cars. You know what they do? They park in country lanes . . ."

"I beg your hard-on?"

"I'd just hate to see a sweet kid like Libby getting into trouble. If you know what I mean?"

Duddy told us about Japanese girls and how they jiggled themselves in swinging hammocks. Nobody believed him.

"I've got the book it's written in," he insisted, "and I'm willing to rent it out."

"Hey," Stan said, "you know why Jewish girls have to wear two-piece bathing suits?"

Nobody knew.

"Mustn't mix the milk with the meat."

"Very funny," Duddy said. "Now deal the cards."

"I'll tell you something that's a fact," Arty said. "Monks never go out with dames. For all their lives – "

"Monks are Catholics, you jerk."

Once poker palled on us, we began to frequent St. Catherine Street on Saturday nights, strutting up and down the neon-lit street in gangs, stopping here for a hot dog and there to play the pinball machines, but never forgetting our primary purpose, which was to taunt the girls as they came strolling past. We tried the Palais d'Or a couple of times, just to see what we could pick up. "Whatever you do," Duddy warned us beforehand, "never give them your right name." But most of the girls shrugged us off. "Send round your older brother, sonny." So we began to go to Belmont Park, hoping to root out younger, more available girls. We danced to the music of Mark Kenny and His Western Gentlemen and at least had some fun in the horror houses and on the rides. We took to playing snooker a good deal.

"A poolroom bum," my father said. "Is that why I'm educating you?"

Then I fell in love.

Zelda was an Outremont girl with a lovely golden head and long dark eyelashes. The night before our first date I consulted *The Art Of Kissing* on HOW TO KISS GIRLS WITH DIFFERENT SIZES OF MOUTHS.

Another question which must be settled at this time concerns the size of the kissee's mouth. Where the girl's mouth is of the tiny rosebud type, then one need not worry about what to do. However, there are many girls whose lips are broad and generous, whose lips are on the order of Joan Crawford's, for instance. The technique in kissing such lips is different. For, were one to allow his lips to remain centered, there would be wide expanses of lips untouched and, therefore, wasted. In such cases, instead of remaining adhered to the centre of the lips, the young man should lift up his lips a trifle and begin to travel around the girl's lips, stopping a number of times to drop a firm kiss in passing. When you have made a complete round of the lips, return immediately to the center bud and feast there. Sip the kissee's honey.

I took Zelda to a "Y" dance and afterwards, outside her house, I attempted to kiss her broad and generous lips.

"I thought," Zelda said, withdrawing stiffly, "you were a more serious type."

And so once more Duddy had to find me dates. One or another of his endless spill of girls always had a cousin with thick glasses – "She's really lots of fun, you know," – or a kid sister – "Honestly, with high heels she looks sixteen."

Some Grist for
Mervyn's Mill

Some Grist for
Mervyn's Mill

Mervyn Kaplansky stepped out of
the rain on a dreary Saturday afternoon in August to inquire
about our back bedroom.

"It's twelve dollars a week," my father said, "payable in
advance."

Mervyn set down forty-eight dollars on the table. Astonished, my father retreated a step. "What's the rush-rush?
Look around first. Maybe you won't like it here."

"You believe in electricity?"

There were no lights on in the house. "We're not the kind
to skimp," my father said. "But we're orthodox here. Today
is *shabus*."

"No, no, no. Between people."

"What are you? A wise-guy."

"I do. And as soon as I came in here I felt the right
vibrations. Hi, kid." Mervyn grinned breezily at me, but the
hand he mussed my hair with was shaking. "I'm going to
love it here."

My father watched, disconcerted but too intimidated to protest, as Mervyn sat down on the bed, bouncing a little to try the mattress. "Go get your mother right away," he said to me.

Fortunately, she had just entered the room. I didn't want to miss anything.

"Meet your new roomer," Mervyn said, jumping up.

"Hold your horses." My father hooked his thumbs in his suspenders. "What do you do for a living?" he asked.

"I'm a writer."

"With what firm?"

"No, no, no. For myself. I'm a creative artist."

My father could see at once that my mother was enraptured and so, reconciled to yet another defeat, he said, "Haven't you any . . . things?"

"When Oscar Wilde entered the United States and they asked him if he had anything to declare, he said, 'Only my genius.'"

My father made a sour face.

"My things are at the station," Mervyn said, swallowing hard. "May I bring them over?"

"Bring."

Mervyn returned an hour or so later with his trunk, several suitcases, and an assortment of oddities that included a piece of driftwood, a wine bottle that had been made into a lamp base, a collection of pebbles, a twelve-inch-high replica of Rodin's *The Thinker*, a bull-fight poster, a Karsh portrait of G.B.S., innumerable notebooks, a ball-point pen with a built-in flashlight, and a framed cheque for fourteen dollars and eighty-five cents from the *Family Herald & Weekly Star*.

"Feel free to borrow any of our books," my mother said.

"Well, thanks. But I try not to read too much now that I'm a wordsmith myself. I'm afraid of being influenced, you see."

Mervyn was a short, fat boy with curly black hair, warm

wet eyes, and an engaging smile. I could see his underwear through the triangles of tension that ran from button
to button down his shirt. The last button had probably burst
off. It was gone. Mervyn, I figured, must have been at least
twenty-three years old, but he looked much younger.

"Where did you say you were from?" my father asked.

"I didn't."

Thumbs hooked in his suspenders, rocking on his heels,
my father waited.

"Toronto," Mervyn said bitterly. "Toronto the Good. My
father's a bigtime insurance agent and my brothers are in
ladies' wear. They're in the rat-race. All of them."

"You'll find that in this house," my mother said, "we are
not materialists."

Mervyn slept in – or, as he put it, stocked the un-
conscious – until noon every day. He typed through the
afternoon and then, depleted, slept some more, and usually
typed again deep into the night. He was the first writer I
had ever met and I worshipped him. So did my mother.

"Have you ever noticed his hands," she said, and I thought
she was going to lecture me about his chewed-up fingernails, but what she said was, "They're artist's hands. Your
grandfather had hands like that." If a neighbour dropped in
for tea, my mother would whisper, "We'll have to speak
quietly," and, indicating the tap-tap of the typewriter from
the back bedroom, she'd add, "in there, Mervyn is creating."
My mother prepared special dishes for Mervyn. Soup, she
felt, was especially nourishing. Fish was the best brain food.
She discouraged chocolates and nuts because of Mervyn's
complexion, but she brought him coffee at all hours, and if
a day passed with no sound coming from the back room my
mother would be extremely upset. Eventually, she'd knock
softly on Mervyn's door. "Anything I can get you?" she'd ask.

"It's no use. It just isn't coming today. I go through periods
like that, you know."

Mervyn was writing a novel, his first, and it was about the struggles of our people in a hostile society. The novel's title was, to begin with, a secret between Mervyn and my mother. Occasionally, he read excerpts to her. She made only one correction. "I wouldn't say 'whore'," she said. "It isn't nice, is it? Say 'lady of easy virtue.'" The two of them began to go in for literary discussions. "Shakespeare," my mother would say, "Shakespeare knew everything." And Mervyn, nodding, would reply, "But he stole all his plots. He was a plagiarist." My mother told Mervyn about her father, the rabbi, and the books he had written in Yiddish. "At his funeral," she told him, "they had to have six motorcycle policemen to control the crowds." More than once my father came home from work to find the two of them still seated at the kitchen table, and his supper wasn't ready or he had to eat a cold plate. Flushing, stammering apologies, Mervyn would flee to his room. He was, I think, the only man who was ever afraid of my father, and this my father found very heady stuff. He spoke gruffly, even profanely in Mervyn's presence, and called him Moitle behind his back. But, when you come down to it, all my father had against Meryvn was the fact that my mother no longer baked potato kugel. (Starch was bad for Mervyn.) My father began to spend more of his time playing cards at Tansky's Cigar & Soda, and when Mervyn fell behind with the rent, he threatened to take action.

"But you can't trouble him now," my mother said, "when he's in the middle of his novel. He works so hard. He's a genius maybe."

"He's peanuts, or what's he doing here?"

I used to fetch Mervyn cigarettes and headache tablets from the drugstore round the corner. On some days when it wasn't coming, the two of us would play casino and Mervyn, at his breezy best, used to wisecrack a lot. "What would you say," he said, "if I told you I aim to out-Emile Zola?" Once he let me read one of his stories, *Was The Champ A Chump?*, that had been printed in magazines in Australia and South Africa. I told him that I wanted to be a writer too. "Kid," he said, "a word from the wise. Never become a wordsmith. Digging ditches would be easier."

From the day of his arrival Mervyn had always worked hard, but what with his money running low he was now so determined to get his novel done, that he seldom went out any more. Not even for a stroll. My mother felt this was bad for his digestion. So she arranged a date with Molly Rosen. Molly, who lived only three doors down the street, was the best looker on St. Urbain, and my mother noticed that for weeks now Mervyn always happened to be standing by the window when it was time for Molly to pass on the way home from work. "Now you go out," my mother said, "and enjoy. You're still a youngster. The novel can wait for a day."

"But what does Molly want with me?"

"She's crazy to meet you. For weeks now she's been asking questions."

Mervyn complained that he lacked a clean shirt, he pleaded a headache, but my mother said, "Don't be afraid she won't eat you." All at once Mervyn's tone changed. He tilted his head cockily. "Don't wait up for me," he said.

Mervyn came home early. "What happened?" I asked.

"I got bored."

"*With* Molly?"

"Molly's an insect. Sex is highly over-estimated, you know. It also saps an artist's creative energies."

But when my mother came home from her Talmud Torah meeting and discovered that Mervyn had come home so early she felt that she had been personally affronted. Mrs. Rosen was summoned to tea.

"It's a Saturday night," she said, "she puts on her best dress, and that cheapskate where does he take her? To sit on the mountain. Do you know that she turned down three other boys, including Ready-To-Wear's *only* son, because you made such a *gedille*?"

"With dumb-bells like Ready-to-Wear she can have dates any night of the week. Mervyn's a creative artist."

"On a Saturday night to take a beautiful young thing to sit on the mountain. From those benches you can get piles."

"Don't be disgusting."

"She's got on her dancing shoes and you know what's for him a date? To watch the people go by. He likes to make up stories about them he says. You mean it breaks his heart to part with a dollar."

"To bring up your daughter to be a gold-digger. For shame."

"All right. I wasn't going to blab, but if that's how you feel – modern men and women, he told her, experiment *before* marriage. And right there on the bench he tried dirty filthy things with her. He . . ."

"Don't draw me no pictures. If I know your Molly he didn't have to try so hard."

"How dare you! She went out with him it was a favour for the marble cake recipe. The dirty piker he asked her to marry him he hasn't even got a job. She laughed in his face."

Mervyn denied that he had tried any funny stuff with Molly – he had too much respect for womankind, he said – but after my father heard that he had come home so early he no longer teased Mervyn when he stood by the window to watch Molly pass. He even resisted making wisecracks when Molly's kid brother returned Mervyn's thick letters unopened. Once, he tried to console Mervyn. "With a towel over the face," he said gruffly, "one's the same as another."

Mervyn's cheeks reddened. He coughed. And my father turned away, disgusted.

"Make no mistake," Mervyn said with a sudden jaunty smile. "You're talking to a boy who's been around. We pen-pushers are notorious lechers."

Mervyn soon fell behind with the rent again and my father began to complain.

"You can't trouble him now," my mother said. "He's in agony. It isn't coming today."

"Yeah, sure. The trouble is there's something coming to me."

"Yesterday he read me a chapter from his book. It's so beautiful you could die." My mother told him that F. J. Kugelman, the Montreal correspondent of *The Jewish Daily Forward*, had looked at the book. "He says Mervyn is a very deep writer."

"Kugelman's for the birds. If Mervyn's such a big writer, let him make me out a cheque for the rent. That's my kind of reading, you know."

"Give him one week more. Something will come through for him, I'm sure."

My father waited another week, counting off the days. "E-Day minus three today," he'd say. "Anything come through for the genius?" Nothing, not one lousy dime, came through for Mervyn. In fact he had secretly borrowed from my mother for the postage to send his novel to a publisher in New York. "E-Day minus one today," my father said. And then, irritated because he had yet to be asked what the E stood for, he added, "E for *E*viction."

On Friday my mother prepared an enormous potato kugel. But when my father came home, elated, the first thing he said was, "Where's Mervyn?"

"Can't you wait until after supper, even?"

Mervyn stepped softly into the kitchen. "You want me?" he asked.

My father slapped a magazine down on the table. *Liberty*. He opened it at a short story titled *A Doll For The Deacon*. "Mel Kane, Jr.," he said, "isn't that your literary handle?"

"His *nom-de-plume*," my mother said.

"Then the story is yours." My father clapped Mervyn on the back. "Why didn't you tell me you were a writer? I thought you were a . . . well, a fruitcup. You know what I mean. A long-hair."

"Let me see that," my mother said.

Absently, my father handed her the magazine. "You mean to say," he said, "you made all that up out of your own head?"

Mervyn nodded. He grinned. But he could see that my mother was displeased.

"It's a top-notch story," my father said. Smiling, he turned to my mother. "All the time I thought he was a sponger. A poet. He's a writer. Can you beat that?" He laughed, delighted. "Excuse me," he said, and he went to wash his hands.

"Here's your story, Mervyn," my mother said. "I'd rather not read it."

Mervyn lowered his head.

"But you don't understand, Maw. Mervyn has to do that sort of stuff. For the money. He's got to eat too, you know."

My mother reflected briefly. "A little tip, then," she said to Mervyn. "Better he doesn't know why . . . well, you understand."

"Sure I do."

At supper my father said, "Hey, what's your novel called, Mr. Kane?"

"The DIRTY JEWS."

"*Are you crazy?*"

"It's an ironic title," my mother said.

"Wow! It sure is."

"I want to throw the lie back in their ugly faces," Mervyn said.

"Yeah. Yeah, sure." My father invited Mervyn to Tansky's to meet the boys. "In one night there," he said, "you can pick up enough material for a book."

"I don't think Mervyn is interested."

Mervyn, I could see, looked dejected. But he didn't dare antagonize my mother. Remembering something he had once told me, I said, "To a creative writer every experience is welcome."

"Yes, that's true," my mother said. "I hadn't thought of it like that."

So my father, Mervyn and I set off together. My father showed *Liberty* to all of Tansky's regulars. While Mervyn lit one cigarette off another, coughed, smiled foolishly and coughed again, my father introduced him as the up-and-coming writer.

"If he's such a big writer what's he doing on St. Urbain Street?"

My father explained that Mervyn had just finished his first novel. "When that comes out," he said, "this boy will be batting in the major leagues."

The regulars looked Mervyn up and down. His suit was shiny.

"You must understand," Mervyn said, "that, at the best of times, it's difficult for an artist to earn a living. Society is naturally hostile to us."

"So what's so special? I'm a plumber. Society isn't hostile to me, but I've got the same problem. Listen here, it's hard for anybody to earn a living."

"You don't get it," Mervyn said, retreating a step. "*I'm* in rebellion against society."

Tansky moved away, disgusted. "Gorki, there was a writer. This boy. . . ."

Molly's father thrust himself into the group surrounding Mervyn. "You wrote a novel," he asked, "it's true?"

"It's with a big publisher in New York right now," my father said.

"You should remember," Takifman said menacingly, "only to write good things about the Jews."

Shapiro winked at Mervyn. The regulars smiled, some

shyly, others hopeful, believing. Mervyn looked back at them solemnly "It is my profound hope," he said, "that in the years to come our people will have every reason to be proud of me."

Segal stood Mervyn for a Pepsi and a sandwich. "Six months from now," he said, "I'll be saying I knew you when. . . ."

Mervyn whirled around on his counter stool. "I'm going to out-Emile Zola," he said. He shook with laughter.

"Do you think there's going to be another war?" Perlman asked.

"Oh, lay off," my father said. "Give the man air. No wisdom outside of office hours, eh, Mervyn?"

Mervyn slapped his knees and laughed some more. Molly's father pulled him aside. "You wrote this story," he said, holding up *Liberty*, "and don't lie because I'll find you out."

"Yeah," Mervyn said, "I'm the grub-streeter who knocked that one off. But it's my novel that I really care about."

"You know who I am? I'm Molly's father. Rosen. Put it there, Mervyn. There's nothing to worry. You leave everything to me."

My mother was still awake when we got home. Alone at the kitchen table. "You were certainly gone a long time," she said to Mervyn.

"Nobody forced him to stay."

"He's too polite," my mother said, slipping her tooled leather bookmark between the pages of *Wuthering Heights*. "He wouldn't tell you when he was bored by such common types."

"Hey," my father said, remembering. "Hey, Mervyn. Can you beat that Takifman for a character?"

Mervyn started to smile, but my mother sighed and he looked away. "It's time I hit the hay," he said.

"Well," my father pulled down his suspenders. "If anyone

wants to use the library let him speak now or forever hold his peace."

"*Please, Sam.* You only say things like that to disgust me. I know that."

My father went into Mervyn's room. He smiled a little. Mervyn waited, puzzled. My father rubbed his forehead. He pulled his ear. "Well, I'm not a fool. You should know that. Life does things to you, but . . ."

"It certainly does, Mr. Hersh."

"You won't end up a zero like me. So I'm glad for you. Well, good night."

But my father did not go to bed immediately. Instead, he got out his collection of pipes, neglected all these years, and sat down at the kitchen table to clean and restore them. And, starting the next morning, he began to search out and clip items in the newspapers, human interest stories with a twist, that might be exploited by Mervyn. When he came home from work – early, he had not stopped off at Tansky's – my father did not demand his supper right off but, instead, went directly to Mervyn's room. I could hear the two men talking in low voices. Finally, my mother had to disturb them. Molly was on the phone.

"Mr. Kaplansky. Mervyn. Would you like to take me out on Friday night? I'm free."

Mervyn didn't answer.

"We could watch the people go by. Anything you say, Mervyn."

"Did your father put you up to this?"

"What's the diff? You wanted to go out with me. Well, on Friday, I'm free."

"I'm sorry. I can't do it."

"Don't you like me any more?"

"I sure do. And the attraction is more than merely sexual. But if we go out together it will have to be because you so desire it."

"Mervyn, if you don't take me out on Friday he won't let me out to the dance Saturday night with Solly. Please, Mervyn."

"Sorry. But I must answer in the negative."

Mervyn told my mother about the telephone conversation and immediately she said, "You did right." But a few days later, she became tremendously concerned about Mervyn. He no longer slept in each morning. Instead, he was the first one up in the house, to wait by the window for the postman. After he had passed, however, Mervyn did not settle down to work. He'd wander sluggishly about the house or go out for a walk. Usually, Mervyn ended up at Tansky's. My father would be waiting there.

"You know," Sugarman said, "many amusing things have happened to me in my life. It would make *some* book."

The men wanted to know Mervyn's opinion of Sholem Asch, the red menace, and ungrateful children. They teased him about my father. "To hear him tell it you're a guaranteed genius."

"Well," Mervyn said, winking, blowing on his fingernails and rubbing them against his jacket lapel, "Who knows?"

But Molly's father said, "I read in the *Gazette* this morning where Hemingway was paid a hundred thousand dollars to make a movie from *one* story. A complete book must be worth at least five short stories. Wouldn't you say?"

And Mervyn, coughing, clearing his throat, didn't answer, but walked off quickly. His shirt collar, too highly starched, cut into the back of his hairless, reddening neck. When I caught up with him, he told me, "No wonder so many artists have been driven to suicide. Nobody understands us. We're not in the rat-race."

Molly came by at seven-thirty on Friday night.

"Is there something I can do for you?" my mother asked.

"I'm here to see Mr. Kaplansky. I believe he rents a room here."

"Better to rent out a room than give fourteen ounces to the pound."

"If you are referring to my father's establishment then I'm sorry he can't give credit to everybody."

"We pay cash everywhere. Knock wood."

"I'm sure. Now, may I see Mr. Kaplansky, *if you don't mind?*"

"He's still dining. But I'll inquire."

Molly didn't wait. She pushed past my mother into the kitchen. Her eyes were a little puffy. It looked to me like she had been crying. "Hi," she said. Molly wore her soft black hair in an upsweep. Her mouth was painted very red.

"Siddown," my father said. "Make yourself homely." Nobody laughed. "It's a joke," he said.

"Are you ready, Mervyn?"

Mervyn fiddled with his fork. "I've got work to do tonight," he said.

"I'll put up a pot of coffee for you right away."

Smiling thinly, Molly pulled back her coat, took a deep breath, and sat down. She had to perch on the edge of the chair either because of her skirt or that it hurt her to sit. "About the novel," she said, smiling at Mervyn, "congrats."

"But it hasn't even been accepted by a publisher yet."

"It's good, isn't it?"

"Of course it's good," my mother said.

"Then what's there to worry? Come on," Molly said, rising. "Let's skidaddle."

We all went to the window to watch them go down the street together.

"Look at her how she's grabbing his arm," my mother said. "Isn't it digusting?"

"You lost by a т.к.о.," my father said.

"*Thanks*," my mother said, and she left the room.

My father blew on his fingers. "Whew," he said. We continued to watch by the window. "I'll bet you she sharp-

ens them on a grindstone every morning to get them so
pointy, and he's such a shortie he wouldn't even have to
bend over to . . ." My father sat down, lit his pipe, and
opened *Liberty* at Mervyn's story. "You know, Mervyn's not
that special a guy. Maybe it's not as hard as it seems to write
a story."

"Digging ditches would be easier," I said.

My father took me to Tansky's for a coke. Drumming
his fingers on the counter, he answered questions about
Mervyn. "Well, it has to do with this thing . . . The Muse.
On some days, with the Muse, he works better. But on other
days . . ." My father addressed the regulars with a daring
touch of condescension; I had never seen him so assured
before. "Well, that depends. But he says Hollywood is very
corrupt."

Mervyn came home shortly after midnight.

"I want to give you a word of advice," my mother said.
"That girl comes from very common people. You can do
better, you know."

My father cracked his knuckles. He didn't look at
Mervyn.

"You've got your future career to think of. You must
choose a mate who won't be an embarrassment in the better
circles."

"Or still better stay a bachelor," my father said.

"Nothing more dreadful can happen to a person," my
mother said, "than to marry somebody who doesn't share
his interests."

"Play the field a little," my father said, drawing on his
pipe.

My mother looked into my father's face and laughed.
My father's voice fell to a whisper. "You get married too
young," he said, "and you live to regret it."

My mother laughed again. Her eyes were wet.

"I'm not the kind to stand by idly," Mervyn said, "while
you insult Miss Rosen's good name."

My father, my mother, looked at Mervyn as if surprised by his presence. Mervyn retreated, startled. *"I mean that,"* he said.

"Just who do you think you're talking to?" my mother said. She looked sharply at my father.

"Hey, there," my father said.

"I hope," my mother said, "success isn't giving you a swelled head."

"Success won't change me. I'm steadfast. But you are intruding into my personal affairs. Good night."

My father seemed both dismayed and a little pleased that someone had spoken up to my mother.

"And just what's ailing you?" my mother asked.

"Me? Nothing."

"If you could only see yourself. At your age. A pipe."

"According to the *Digest* it's safer than cigarettes."

"You know absolutely nothing about people. Mervyn would never be rude to me. It's only his artistic temperament coming out."

My father waited until my mother had gone to bed and then he slipped into Mervyn's room. "Hi." He sat down on the edge of Mervyn's bed. "Tell me to mind my own business if you want me to, but . . . well, have you had bad news from New York? The publisher?"

"I'm still waiting to hear from New York."

"Sure," my father said, jumping up. "Sorry. Good night." But he paused briefly at the door. "I've gone out on a limb for you. Please don't let me down."

Molly's father phoned the next morning. "You had a good time Mervyn?"

"Yeah. Yeah, sure."

"Atta boy. That girl she's crazy about you. Like they say she's walking on air."

Molly, they said, had told the other girls in the office at Susy's Smart-Wear that she would probably soon be leaving for, as she put it, tropical climes. Gitel Shalinsky saw her shopping for beach wear on Park Avenue – in November, this – and the rumour was that Mervyn had already accepted a Hollywood offer for his book, a guaranteed best-seller. A couple of days later a package came for Mervyn. It was his novel. There was a printed form enclosed with it. The publishers felt the book was not for them.

"Tough luck," my father said.

"It's nothing," Mervyn said breezily. "Some of the best wordsmiths going have had their novels turned down six-seven times before a publisher take it. Besides, this outfit wasn't for me in the first place. It's a homosexual company. They only print the pretty-pretty prose boys." Mervyn laughed, he slapped his knees. "I'll send the book off to another publisher today."

My mother made Mervyn his favorite dishes for dinner. "You have real talent," she said to him, "and everything will come to you." Afterwards, Molly came by. Mervyn came home very late this time, but my mother waited up for him all the same.

"I'm invited to eat at the Rosens on Saturday night. Isn't that nice?"

"But I ordered something special from the butcher for us here."

"I'm sorry. I didn't know."

"So now you know. Please yourself, Mervyn. Oh, it's alright. I changed your bed. But you could have told me, you know."

Mervyn locked his hands together to quiet them. "Tell you what, for Christ's sake? There's nothing to tell."

"It's alright, *boyele*," my mother said. "Accidents happen."

Once more my father slipped into Mervyn's room. "It's O.K.," he said, "don't worry about Saturday night. Play around. Work the kinks out. But don't put anything in writing. You might live to regret it."

"I happen to think Molly is a remarkable girl."

"Me too. I'm not as old as you think."

"No, no, no. You don't understand."

My father showed Mervyn some clippings he had saved for him. One news story told of two brothers who had discovered each other by accident after twenty-five years, another was all about a funny day at court. He also gave Mervyn an announcement for the annual Y.H.M.A. *Beacon* short story contest. "I've got an idea for you," he said. "Listen, Mervyn, in the movies . . . well, when Humphrey Bogart, for instance, lights up a Chesterfield or asks for a coke you think he doesn't get a nice little envelope from the companies concerned? Sure he does. Well, your problem seems to be money. So why couldn't you do the same thing in books? Like if your hero has to fly somewhere, for instance, why use an unnamed airline? Couldn't he go TWA because it's the safest, the best, and maybe he picks up a cutie-pie on board? Or if your central character is . . . well, a lush, couldn't he always insist on Seagram's because it's the greatest? Get the idea? I could write, say, TWA, Pepsi, Seagram's and Adam's Hats and find out just how much a book plug is worth to them, and you . . . well, what do you think?"

"I could never do that in a book of mine, that's what I think. It would reflect on my integrity. People would begin to talk, see."

But people had already begun to talk. Molly's kid brother told me Mervyn had made a hit at dinner. His father, he said, had told Mervyn he felt, along with the moderns, that in-laws should not live with young couples, not always, but the climate in Montreal was a real killer for his wife, and if it so happened that he ever had a son-in-law in, let's say, California . . . well, it would be nice to visit . . . and Mervyn agreed that families should be close-knit. Not all the talk was favourable, however. The boys on the street were hostile to Mervyn. An outsider, a Torontonian, they felt, was threatening to carry off our Molly.

"There they go," the boys would say as Molly and Mervyn

walked hand-in-hand past the pool room, "Beauty and the Beast."

"All these years they've been looking, and looking, and looking, and there he is, the missing link."

Mervyn was openly taunted on the street.

"Hey, big writer. Lard-ass. How many periods in a bottle of ink?"

"Shakespeare, come here. How did you get to look like that, or were you paid for the accident?"

But Mervyn assured me that he wasn't troubled by the boys. "The masses," he said, "have always been hostile to the artist. They've driven plenty of our number to self-slaughter, you know. But I can see through them."

His novel was turned down again.

"It doesn't matter," Mervyn said. "There are better publishers."

"But wouldn't they be experts there," my father asked. "I mean maybe . . ."

"Look at this, will you? This time they sent me a personal letter! You know who this is from? It's from one of the greatest editors in all of America."

"Maybe so," my father said uneasily, "but he doesn't want your book."

"He admires my energy and enthusiasm, doesn't he?"

Once more Mervyn mailed off his novel, but this time he did not resume his watch by the window. Mervyn was no longer the same. I don't mean that his face had broken out worse than ever – it had, it's true, only that was probably because he was eating too many starchy foods again – but suddenly he seemed indifferent to his novel's fate. I gave birth, he said, sent my baby out into the world, and now he's on his own. Another factor was that Mervyn had become, as he put it, pregnant once more (he looks it too, one of Tansky's regulars told me): that is to say, he was at work on a new book. My mother interpreted this as a very good sign and she did her utmost to encourage Mervyn. Though she continued to change his sheets just about every other night, she never complained about it. Why, she even pretended this was normal procedure in our house. But Mervyn seemed perpetually irritated and he avoided the type of literary discussion that had formerly given my mother such deep pleasure. Every night now he went out with Molly and there were times when he did not return until four or five in the morning.

And now, curiously enough, it was my father who waited up for Mervyn, or stole out of bed to join him in the kitchen. He would make coffee and take down his prized bottle of apricot brandy. More than once I was wakened by his laughter. My father told Mervyn stories of his father's house, his boyhood, and the hard times that came after. He told Mervyn how his mother-in-law had been bedridden in our house for seven years, and with pride implicit in his every word – a pride that would have amazed and maybe even flattered my mother – he told Mervyn how my mother had tended to the old lady better than any nurse with umpteen diplomas. "To see her now," I heard my father say, "is like night and day. Before the time of the old lady's stroke she was no sour-puss. Well, that's life." He told Mervyn about the first time he had seen my mother, and how she had written him letters with poems by Shelley, Keats and Byron in them, when all the time he had lived only two streets away. But another time I heard my father say, "When I was a young man, you know, there were days on end when I never went to bed. I was so excited. I used to go out and walk the streets better than snooze. I thought if I slept maybe I'd miss something. Now isn't that crazy?" Mervyn muttered a reply. Usually, he seemed weary and self-absorbed. But my father was irrepressible. Listening to him, his tender tone with

Mervyn and the surprise of his laughter, I felt that I had reason to be envious. My father had never talked like that to me or my sister. But I was so astonished to discover this side of my father, it was all so unexpected, that I soon forgot my jealousy.

One night I heard Mervyn tell my father, "Maybe the novel I sent out is no good. Maybe it's just something I had to work out of my system."

"Are you crazy it's no good? I told everyone you were a big writer."

"It's the apricot brandy talking," Mervyn said breezily. "I was only kidding you."

But Mervyn had his problems. I heard from Molly's kid brother that Mr. Rosen had told him he was ready to retire. "Not that I want to be a burden to anybody," he had said. Molly had begun to take all the movie magazines available at Tansky's. "So that when I meet the stars face to face," she had told Gitel, "I shouldn't put my foot in it, and embarrass Merv."

Mervyn began to pick at his food, and it was not uncommon for him to leap up from the table and rush to the bathroom, holding his hand to his mouth. I discovered for the first time that my mother had bought a rubber sheet for Mervyn's bed. If Mervyn had to pass Tansky's, he no longer stopped to shoot the breeze. Instead, he would hurry past, his head lowered. Once, Segal stopped him. "What's a matter," he said, "you too good for us now?"

Tansky's regulars began to work on my father.

"All of a sudden, your genius there, he's such a B.T.O.," Sugerman said, "that he has no time for us here."

"Let's face it," my father said. "You're zeros. We all are. But my friend Mervyn . . ."

"Don't tell me, Sam. He's full of beans. Baked beans."

My father stopped going to Tansky's altogether. He took to playing solitaire at home.

"What are you doing here?" my mother asked.

"Can't I stay home one night? It's my house too, you know."

"I want the truth, Sam."

"Aw, those guys. You think those cockroaches know what an artist's struggle is?" He hesitated, watching my mother closely. "By them it must be that Mervyn isn't good enough. He's no writer."

"You know," my mother said, "he owes us seven weeks' rent now."

"The first day Mervyn came here," my father said, his eyes half-shut as he held a match to his pipe, "he said there was a kind of electricity between us. Well, I'm not going to let him down over a few bucks."

But something was bothering Mervyn. For that night and the next he did not go out with Molly. He went to the window to watch her pass again and then retreated to his room to do the crossword puzzles.

"Feel like a casino?" I asked.

"I love that girl," Mervyn said. "I adore her."

"I thought everything was O.K., but. I thought you were making time."

"No, no, no. I want to marry her. I told Molly that I'd settle down and get a job if she'd have me."

"Are you crazy? A job? With your talent?"

"That's what she said."

"Aw, let's play casino. It'll take your mind off things."

"She doesn't understand. Nobody does. For me to take a job is not like some ordinary guy taking a job. I'm always studying my own reactions. I want to know how a shipper feels from the inside."

"You mean you'd take a job *as a shipper*?"

"But it's not like I'd really be a shipper. It would look like that from the outside, but I'd really be studying my co-workers all the time. I'm an artist, you know."

"Stop worrying, Mervyn. Tomorrow there'll be a letter begging you for your book."

But the next day nothing came. A week passed. Ten days.

"That's a very good sign," Mervyn said. "It means they are considering my book very carefully."

It got so we all waited around for the postman. Mervyn was aware that my father did not go to Tansky's any more and that my mother's friends had begun to tease her. Except for his endless phone calls to Molly he hardly ever came out of his room. The phone calls were futile. Molly wouldn't speak to him.

One evening my father returned from work, his face flushed. "Son-of-a-bitch," he said, "that Rosen he's a cock-roach. You know what he's saying? He wouldn't have in his family a faker or a swindler. He said you were not a writer, Mervyn, but garbage." My father started to laugh. "But I trapped him for a liar. You know what he said? That you were going to take a job as a shipper. Boy, did I ever tell him."

"What did you say?" my mother asked.

"I told him good. Don't you worry. When I lose my temper, you know. . . ."

"Maybe it wouldn't be such a bad idea for Mervyn to take a job. Better than go into debt he could – "

"You shouldn't have bragged about me to your friends so much," Mervyn said to my mother. "I didn't ask it."

"*I'm* a braggard? You take that back. You owe me an apology, I think. After all, *you're* the one who said you were such a big writer."

"My talent is unquestioned. I have stacks of letters from important people and – "

"I'm waiting for an apology, Sam?"

"I have to be fair. I've seen some of the letters, so that's true. But that's not to say Emily Post would approve of Mervyn calling you a – "

"My husband was right the first time. When he said you were a sponger, Mervyn."

"Don't worry," Mervyn said, turning to my father. "You'll get your rent back no matter what. Good night."

I can't swear to it. I may have imagined it. But when I got up to go to the toilet late that night it seemed to me that I heard Mervyn sobbing in his room. Anyway, the next morning the postman rang the bell and Mervyn came back with a package and a letter.

"Not again," my father said.

"No. This happens to be a letter from the most important publisher in the United States. They are going to pay me two thousand five hundred dollars for my book in advance against royalties."

"Hey. Lemme see that."

"Don't you trust me?"

"Of course we do." My mother hugged Mervyn. "All the time I knew you had it in you."

"This calls for a celebration," my father said, going to get the apricot brandy.

My mother went to phone Mrs. Fisher. "Oh, Ida, I just called to say I'll be able to bake for the bazaar after all. No, nothing new here. Oh, I almost forgot. Remember Mervyn you were saying he was nothing but a little twerp? Well, he just got a fantastic offer for his book from a publisher in New York. No, I'm only allowed to say it runs into four figures. Excited? That one. I'm not even sure he'll accept."

My father grabbed the phone to call Tansky's.

"One minute. Hold it. Couldn't we keep quiet about this, and have a private sort of celebration?"

My father got through to the store. "Hello, Sugarman?

Everybody come over here. Drinks on the house. Why, of
Korsakov. No, wise-guy. She certainly isn't. At her age? It's
Mervyn. He's considering a five thousand dollar offer just to
sign a contract for his book."

The phone rang an instant after my father had hung up.
"Well, hello Mrs. Rosen," my mother said. "Well, thank
you. I'll give him the message. No, no, why should I have
anything against you we've been neighbours for years. No.
Certainly not. It wasn't *me* you called a piker. Your Molly
didn't laugh in my face."

Unnoticed, Mervyn sat down on the sofa. He held his
head in his hands.

"There's the doorbell," my father said.

"I think I'll lie down for a minute. Excuse me."

By the time Mervyn came out of his room again many
of Tansky's regulars had arrived. "If it had been up to me,"
my father said, "none of you would be here. But Mervyn's
not the type to hold grudges."

Molly's father elbowed his way through the group surrounding Mervyn. "I want you to know," he said, "that I'm
proud of you today. There's nobody I'd rather have for a
son-in-law."

"You're sort of hurrying things. Aren't you?"

"What? Didn't you propose to her a hundred times she
wouldn't have you? And now I'm standing here to tell you
alright and you're beginning with the shaking in the pants.
This I don't like."

Everybody turned to stare. There was some good natured
laughter.

"You wrote her such letters they still bring a blush to my
face — "

"But they came back unopened."

Molly's father shrugged and Mervyn's face turned grey
as a pencil eraser.

"But you listen here," Rosen said. "For Molly, if you don't
mind, it isn't necessary for me to go begging."

"Here she is," somebody said.

The regulars moved in closer.

"Hi," Molly smelled richly of Lily of the Valley. You could see the outlines of her bra through her sweater (both were in Midnight Black, from Susy's Smart-Wear). Her tartan skirt was held together by an enormous gold-plated safety pin. "Hi, doll." She rushed up to Mervyn and kissed him. "Maw just told me." Molly turned to the others, her smile radiant. "Mr. Kaplansky has asked for my hand in matrimony. We are engaged."

"Congratulations!" Rosen clapped Mervyn on the back. "The very best to you both."

There were whoops of approval all around.

"When it comes to choosing a bedroom set you can't go wrong with my son-in-law Lou."

"I hope," Takifman said sternly, "yours will be a kosher home."

"Some of the biggest crooks in town only eat kosher and I don't mind saying that straight to your face, Takifman."

"He's right, you know. And these days the most important thing with young couples is that they should be sexually compatible."

Mervyn, surrounded by the men, looked over their heads for Molly. He spotted her trapped in another circle in the far corner of the room. Molly was eating a banana. She smiled at Mervyn, she winked.

"Don't they make a lovely couple?"

"Twenty years ago they said the same thing about us. Does that answer your question?"

Mervyn was drinking heavily. He looked sick.

"Hey," my father said, his glass spilling over, "tell me, Segal, what goes in hard and stiff and comes out soft and wet?"

"Oh, for Christ's sake," I said. "Chewing gum. It's as old as the hills."

"You watch out," my father said. "You're asking for it."

"You know," Miller said. "I could do with something to eat."

My mother moved silently and tight-lipped among the guests collecting glasses just as soon as they were put down.

"I'll tell you what," Rosen said in a booming voice, "let's all go over to my place for a decent feed and some schnapps."

Our living room emptied more quickly than it had filled.

"Where's your mother?" my father asked, puzzled.

I told him she was in the kitchen and we went to get her. "Come on," my father said, "let's go to the Rosens."

"And who, may I ask, will clean up the mess you and your friends made here?"

"It won't run away."

"You have no pride."

"Oh, please. Don't start. Not today."

"Drunkard."

"Ray Milland, that's me. Hey, what's that coming out of the wall? A bat."

"That poor innocent boy is being railroaded into a marriage he doesn't want and you just stand there."

"Couldn't you enjoy yourself *just once*?"

"You didn't see his face how scared he was? I thought he'd faint."

"Who ever got married he didn't need a little push? Why, I remember when I was a young man – "

"You go, Sam. Do me a favour. Go to the Rosen's."

My father sent me out of the room.

"I'm not," he began, "well, I'm not always happy with you. Not day in and day out. I'm telling you straight."

"When I needed you to speak up for me you couldn't. Today courage comes in bottles. Do me a favour, Sam. Go."

"I wasn't going to go and leave you alone. I was going to stay. But if that's how you feel. . . ."

My father returned to the living room to get his jacket. I jumped up.

"Where are *you* going?" he asked.

"To the party."

"You stay here with your mother you have no consideration."

"God damn it."

"You heard me," But my father paused for a moment at the door. Thumbs hooked in his suspenders, rocking to and fro on his heels, he raised his head so high his chin jutted out incongruously. "I wasn't always your father. I was a young man once."

"So?"

"Did you know," he said, one eye half-shut, "that LIVE spelled backwards is EVIL?"

I woke at three in the morning when I heard a chair crash in the living room; somebody fell, and this was followed by the sound of sobbing. It was Mervyn. Dizzy, wretched and bewildered. He sat on the floor with a glass in his hand. When he saw me coming he raised his glass. "The wordsmith's bottled enemy," he said, grinning.

"When you getting married?"

He laughed. I laughed too.

"I'm not getting married."

"Wha'?"

"Sh."

"But I thought you were crazy about Molly?"

"I was. I am no longer." Mervyn rose, he tottered over to the window.

"Have you ever looked up at the stars," he said, "and felt how small and unimportant we are?"

It hadn't occurred to me before.

"Nothing really matters. In terms of eternity our lives are shorter than a cigarette puff. Hey," he said. "Hey!" He took out his pen with the built-in flashlight and wrote something in his notebook. "For a writer," he said, "everything is grist to the mill. Nothing is humiliating."

"But what about Molly?"

"She's an insect. I told you the first time. All she wanted

was my kudos. My fame . . . If you're really going to become a wordsmith remember one thing. The world is full of ridicule while you struggle. But once you've made it the glamour girls will come crawling."

He had begun to cry again. "Want me to sit with you for a while," I said.

"No. Go to bed. Leave me alone."

The next morning at breakfast my parents weren't talking. My mother's eyes were red and swollen and my father was in a forbidding mood. A telegram came for Mervyn.

"It's from New York," he said. "They want me right away. There's an offer for my book from Hollywood and they need me."

"You don't say?"

Mervyn thrust the telegram at my father. "Here," he said. "You read it."

"Take it easy. All I said was . . ." But my father read the telegram all the same. "Son-of-a-bitch," he said. "Hollywood."

We helped Mervyn pack.

"Shall I get Molly?" my father asked.

"No. I'll only be gone for a few days. I want to surprise her."

We all went to the window to wave. Just before he got into the taxi Mervyn looked up at us, he looked for a long while, but he didn't wave, and of course we never saw him again. A few days later a bill came for the telegram. It had been sent from our house. "I'm not surprised," my mother said.

My mother blamed the Rosens for Mervyn's flight, while they held us responsible for what they called their daughter's disgrace. My father put his pipes aside again and naturally he took a terrible ribbing at Tansky's. About a month later five dollar bills began to arrive from Toronto. They came sporadically until Mervyn had paid up all his back rent. But he never answered any of my father's letters.

The War, Chaverim,
and After

The War, Chaverim, and After

Blumberg, our fourth grade teacher, was a militant Zionist.

"How did we get arms in Eretz? Why, we bought them from the British. We'd pretend somebody was dead, fill a coffin with rifles, and bury it against . . . the right moment."

If we responded to this tale of cunning with yawns or maybe two fingers held up to signify disbelief, it was not that we weren't impressed. It was simply that Blumberg, a refugee from Poland, heaped a vengeful amount of homework on us and we thrived on putting him down. Blumberg fed us on frightening stories of anti-semitic outrages. Life would be sour for us. We were doomed to suffer the malice of the Gentiles. But I wasn't scared because I had no intention of becoming a Jew like Blumberg, with a foolish accent, an eye for a bargain, and a habit, clearly unsanitary, of licking his thumb before turning a page of the *Aufbau*. I was a real Canadian and could understand people not liking Blumberg, maybe even finding him funny. So did I. Blumberg had

lived in Palestine for a while and despised the British army.
I didn't. How could I? *In Which We Serve* was in its ump-
teenth week at the Orpheum. Cousins and uncles were with
the Canadian army in Sussex, training for the invasion.

War. "Praise the Lord," my father sang, demanding more
baked beans, "and pass the ammuntion." My Cousin Jerry
wore a Red Cross Blood Donor's badge. I collected salvage.

The war meant if we ate plenty of carrots we would see
better in the dark, like R.A.F. night fighters. V stood for
Victory. Paul Lukas was watching out for us on the Rhine.
Signs in all our cigar stores and delicatessens warned
chassids, pressers, dry goods wholesalers, tailors, and *mela-
muds* against loose talk about troop movements. University
students, my Cousin Jerry among them, went out west to
harvest the wheat. My uncles, who bought two dogs to
guard their junk yard, named them Adolf and Benito. Arty,
Gas. Hershey, Duddy and I gave up collecting hockey
cards for the duration and instead became experts on aircraft recognition. Come recess we were forever flashing cards
with airplane silhouettes at each other. I learned to tell a
Stuka from a Spitfire.

One of the first to enlist was killed almost immediately.
Benjy Trachstein joined the R.C.A.F. and the first time he
went up with an instructor in a Harvard trainer the aeroplane broke apart, crashed on the outskirts of Montreal, and
Benjy burned to death. Charred to the bone. At the funeral,
my father said, "It's kismet – fate. When your time comes,
your times comes."

Mrs. Trachstein went out of her mind and Benjy's father,
a grocer, became a withering reproach to everyone. "When
is your black-marketeer of a son going to join up?" he asked
one mother and to another he said, "How much did it cost
you the doctor to keep your boy out of the army?"

We began to avoid Trachstein's grocery, the excuse
being he never washed his hands any more: it was enough
to turn your stomach to take a pound of cheese from him or

to eat a herring he had touched. It was also suspected that Trachtstein was the one who had written those anonymous letters reporting other stores in the neighbourhood to the Wartime Prices & Trade Board. The letters were a costly nuisance. An inspector always followed up because there could be twenty dollars or maybe even a case of whisky in it for him.

Benjy's wasted death was brandished at any boy on the street hot-headed enough to want to enlist. Still, they volunteered. Some because they were politically-conscious, others because boredom made them reckless. One Saturday morning Gordie Roth, a long fuzzy-haired boy with watery blue eyes, turned up at the Young Israel synagogue in an officer's uniform. His father broke down and sobbed and shuffled out of the *shul* without a word to his son. Those who had elected to stay on at McGill, thereby gaining an exemption from military service, were insulted by Gordie's gesture. It was one thing for a dental graduate to accept a commission in the medical corps, something else again for a boy to chuck law school for the infantry. Privately the boys said Gordie wasn't such a hero, he had been bound to flunk out at McGill anyway. Garber's boy, a psychology major, had plenty to say about the death-wish. But Fay Katz wrinkled her nose and laughed spitefully at him. "You know what that is down your back," she said, "a yellow stripe."

Mothers who had once bragged about their children's health, making any childhood illness seem a shameful show of weakness, now cherished nothing in their young so greedily as flat feet, astigmatism, a heart murmur, or a nice little rupture. After a month in camp with the university army training corps my Cousin Jerry limped home with raw bleeding feet and jaundice. A Sergeant McCormick had called him a hard-assed kike.

"Why should we fight for them, the fascists," my father said.

"The poor boy, what he's been through," my mother said.

Hershey had a brother overseas. Arty's American cousin was in the marines. I was bitterly disappointed in Cousin Jerry and couldn't look him in the eye.

One evening my father read us an item from the front page of the *Star*. A luftwaffe pilot, shot down over London, had been given a blood transfusion. "There you are, old chap," the British doctor said. "Now you've got some good Jewish blood in you." My father scratched his head thoughtfully before turning the page and I could see that he was immensely pleased.

Only Tansky, who ran the corner Cigar & Soda, questioned the integrity of the British war effort. Lots of ships were being sunk in the Battle of the Atlantic, true, but how many people knew that u-boat commanders never torpedoed a ship insured by Lloyd's or that certain German factories were proof against air raids, because of interlocking British directorships?

If Tansky was concerned about capitalist treachery overseas the truth is French Canadians at home gave us much more cause for alarm. Duplessis's *Union Nationale* Party had circulated a pamphlet that showed a coarse old Jew, nose long and mis-shapen as a carrot, retreating into the night with sacks of gold. The caption suggested that Ikey ought to go back to Palestine. Mr. Blumberg, our fourth grade teacher, agreed. "There's only one place for a Jew. Eretz. But you boys are too soft. You know nothing about what it is to be a Jew."

Our parochial school principal was a Zionist of a different order. His affinities were literary. Ahad Ha'am, Bialik, Buber. But I managed to graduate to F.F.H.S. uncontaminated. In fact I doubt that I ever would have become a Zionist if not for Irving.

Irving, who was in my classroom at F.F.H.S., ignored me for months. Then, on the day our report cards came out, he

joined me by the lockers, bouncing a mock punch off my
shoulder. "Congrats," he said.

I looked baffled.

"Well, you're rank two, aren'cha?"

Irving represented everything I admired. He wore a
blazer with IRV printed in gold letters across his broad back
and there was a hockey crest sewn over his heart. He had
fought in the Golden Gloves for the Y.M.H.A. and he was
high scorer on our school basketball team. Whenever Irving
began to dribble shiftily down the court the girls would
squeal, leap up, and shout,

> X_2, Y_2, H_2SO_4,
> Themistocles, Thermopylae, the Peloponnesian War,
> One-two-three-four,
> Who are we for –
> IRVING, OLD BOY!

Irving went in for rakishly pegged trousers and always
carried prophylactics in his billfold.

"How would you like to come down to Habonim with me
tonight? If you like it, maybe you'll join."

"Sure," I said.

The Habonim meeting house was on Jeanne Mance
Street, not far from my grandfather's house, and I recalled
that on Friday nights the old man glowered as the *chaverim*
passed, singing lustily. The fact that it was the sabbath was
all that restrained my grandfather from calling the police to
protest against the racket the *chaverim* kicked up. My grandfather was uncompromisingly orthodox. Switching on lights,
tearing paper, were both forbidden on the sabbath. So late
Friday afternoon it fell to one of my aunts to tear sufficient
toilet paper to see us through *shabbus*; and one of my uncles
had devised a Rube Goldberg type apparatus, the key part

of which was a string attached to a clock that turned off the
toilet and hall lights when the alarm sounded at midnight.

Now I would have to risk passing the house with the
others. Shoving, throwing snowballs, teasing the girls, singing.

    Pa'am achas bochur ya-'za, bochur v'bachura. . . .

Irving, chewing on a matchstick, picked me up after
supper and on the way we called for Hershey and Gas. I was
flattered that Irving had come to my house first, and in the
guise of telling him what fun Hershey and Gas were, I let
him understand that I was a much more desirable boy to
have for a friend.

Walking to Habonim with Irving, Hershey and Gas, became a Friday night ritual that was to continue unbroken
through four years of high school.

The war was done. Cousins and uncles were gradually
coming home.

  – What was it like over there?

  – An education.

We read in the *Star* that in Denver a veteran had run
amuk and shot people down in the street; the *Reader's
Digest* warned us not to ask too many questions, the boys
had been through hell; but on St. Urbain the boys took off
their uniforms, bought new suits, and took up where they
had left off.

IS HITLER REALLY DEAD? was what concerned all of us.
That, and an end to wartime shortages. Sugar, coffee, and
gas, came off the ration list. The Better Business Bureau
warned housewives not to buy soaps or combs from door-to-
door vendors who claimed to be disabled veterans. An in-
trepid reporter walked the length of Calgary's main street in
an s.s. uniform without being stopped once. HAVE WE FORGOT-
TEN WHAT THE BOYS DIED FOR, he wanted to know. Ted Williams was safe, so was Jimmy Stewart. Mackenzie King wrote,

"It affords me much pleasure both personally and as Prime Minister, to add a word of tribute to the record of the services of Canadian Jews in the armed forces in the recent war." Pete Grey, the Toronto Maple Leafs' one-armed player, was made a free agent. A returning veteran took his place in the outfield.

Harry, our group leader in Habonim, had served in the R.C.A.F., where it had been his job to show returned fighter pilots the combat films they had taken. Each time a pilot fired his guns, Harry explained, a camera in the wings took pictures, which was how it could be established if a pilot's claim to a kill was true. Some of the films, he said, showed enemy aircraft bursting into flames. But on the flight home most of the pilots swooped low over German streets to shoot up cyclists for sport. These films would end abruptly – just as the cyclists crumpled.

Hershey's father, gone into the war a scrap dealer, a rotund good natured man whose sporting life had once been confined to cracking peanuts in the Delormier Downs bleachers at Sunday afternoon double-headers, now flew army ordnance corps colonels and their secretaries by chartered aeroplane to his hunting and fishing cabin on a lake in northern Quebec. He emerged as a leading dealer in army surplus trucks, jeeps, and other heavy equipment. Hershey's family moved to Outremont.

Duddy Kravitz drifted away from us too. Calling himself Victory Vendors he bought four peanut machines and set them up on what he had clocked as the busiest corners in the neighbourhood.

Irving and I became inseparable, but his father terrified me.

"You know what you are," Irving's father was fond of saying. "Your father's mistake."

Irving's father was a widower – a wiry grey-haired man with mocking black eyes. He astonished me because he didn't eat kosher and he drank. Not a quick little schnapps with honey cake, head tossed back and eyes immediately

tearing, like my father and the other men at the synagogue
when there was a bar-mitzvah.

– This is quality stuff. The best.

– It warms you right here.

– Smooth.

Irving's father drank Black Horse Ale, bottle after bottle.
He settled in sullenly at the kitchen table, his smile morose,
and suddenly he would call out, "Pull my finger!" If you
did he let out a tremendous burp. Irving's father could fall
asleep at the table, mouth open, a cigarette burning between his stubby blackened fingers. Sometimes he sat with
us on Saturday nights to listen to the hockey broadcasts.
He was a *Canadiens* fan. "You can't beat the Rocket or
Durnan when the chips are down. They're money players.
Real money players – heeeey, here it comes . . ." He lifted
himself gently off the chair. "sbd." A self-satisfied pause.
"Know what that means, kid?"

Irving, holding his nose, would open the window.

"Silent But Deadly."

Another time Irving's father said, "Here," shoving a
finger under my nose. "Smell."

Scared, I had a whiff.

"That's the one that went through the paper."

Irving's father ridiculed Habonim.

"So, little *shmedricks*, what are you going to do? Save the
Jews? Any time the Arabs want they can run them right
into the sea."

On the occasional Friday I was allowed to stay over-
night at Irving's house and the two of us would sit up late
to talk about Eretz.

"I can hardly wait to go," Irving said.

I can no longer remember much about our group meet-
ings on Fridays or the impassioned general meetings on
Sunday afternoons. I can recall catch-words, no more.
Yishuv, White Paper, emancipation, Negev, revisionist,
Aliyah. Pierre Van Paasen was our trusted ally; Koestler,

since *Thieves in the Night*, was despicable. Following our group meetings we all clambered down to the whitewashed cellar to join the girls and dance the hora. I seldom took part, preferring to puff at my newly-acquired pipe on the sidelines, and watch Gitel's breasts heave. Afterwards we spilled exhuberantly on to the street and either continued on to one of the girls' homes to neck or drifted to the Park Bowling Academy.

On Saturdays we listened to speeches about soil redemption, we saw movies glorifying life on the kibbutz. All of us planned to settle in Eretz.

"What's there for a Jew here? Balls all squared."

"Did you hear about Jack Zimmerman's brother? He came third in the province in the matrics and they still won't let him into pre-med school."

Early Sunday morning we were out ringing door bells for the Jewish National Fund, shaking tin boxes under uprooted sleepy faces, righteously demanding quarters, dimes, and nickels that would help reclaim the desert, buy arms for Hagana and, incidently, yield thirty-five cents off the top – enough for the matinée at the Rialto. We licked envelopes at Zionist headquarters. Our choir sung at fundraising rallies. And in the summertime those among us who were not working as waiters or shippers went to a camp in a mosquito-ridden Laurentian valley, heard more speakers, studied Hebrew and, in the absence of Arabs, watched out for fishy-looking French Canadians. Our unrivalled hero was the *chalutz*, and I can still see him as he stood on the cover of God knows how many pamphlets, clear-eyed, resolute, a rifle slung over his shoulder and a sickle in his hand.

After the meeting one Friday night Irving pulled me aside. "If my father calls tell him I'm staying at your house tonight."

"Sure," I said, delighted, and I offered to invite Hershey,

Gas, and some of the others over for a blackjack game. Then, looking into Irving's apprehensive face, I suddenly understood. "Oh. Oh, I get you. Where you going, but?"

Irving put a finger to his lips, he gave me a meaningful look. For the first time, I noticed Selma strolling slowly ahead of us down the street. She stopped to contemplate a shop window.

"Go to hell," I said vehemently to Irving, surprising myself.

"You'll do it, but."

"Sure, sure," I said, hurrying off in the opposite direction.

Selma was reputed to be hot stuff – crazy for it, Stan said – but all I saw was a shy dark girl with blue-black hair, a manner that was somewhat withdrawn, and the loveliest breasts imaginable.

"You know what she told me," Hershey said. "She broke it jumping over a fire hydrant when she was a kid. Oi."

Even Arty, who was as short as me with worse pimples, claimed to have necked through *The Jolson Story* three times with Selma.

On Friday, having managed to walk all the way to Habonim without once treading on a sidewalk crack, I asked Selma to come to a dance with me. But she was busy, she said.

On the night of Nov 29, 1947, after the UN approved the partition plan, we gathered at Habonim and marched downtown in a group, waving Israeli flags, flaunting our songs in WASP neighbourhoods, stopping to blow horns and pull down street car wires, until we reached the heart of the city where, as I remember it, we faltered briefly, embarrassed, self-conscious, before we put a halt to traffic by forming in defiant circles and dancing the hora in the middle of the street.

"Who am I?"

"YISROAL."

"Who are you?"

"YISROAL."

"All of us?"

"YISRO-YISRO-YISROAL."

Our group leaders, as well as several of the older *chaverim*, went off to fight for Eretz. I lied about my age and joined the Canadian Reserve Army, thinking how wonderfully ironic it would be to have Canada train me to fight the British, but in the end I relented and decided to finish high school instead.

In the febrile days that followed the proclamation of the State of Israel, we gathered nightly at Habonim to discuss developments in Eretz and at home. A distiguished Jewish doctor was invited to address the Canadian Club. To our astonishment, the doctor said that though he was Jewish he remained, first of all, a Canadian. Israel, he warned, would make for divided loyalties, and he was opposed to the establishment of the new state.

Tansky's regulars were in an uproar.

"He's what you call an assimilationist."

"You'd think what happened in Germany would have taught such people a lesson – once and for all."

Sugarman pointed out that the doctor was already an O.B.E. "My son says he's sucking after something bigger on the next Honours List."

The *Star* printed the complete text of the doctor's speech.

"If Ben Gurion speaks," Takifman said, "maybe they can fit in a paragraph on page thirty-two, but if that *shmock* opens his lousy mouth. . . ."

Punitive action came quickly. The editor of the *Canadian Jewish Eagle* wrote that the Star of David will long outshine the *Star* of Montreal. We collected money so that A. M. Klein, the poet, could reply to the doctor on the radio. We also, I'm sorry to say, took to phoning the doctor at all hours of the night, shouting obscenities at him, and hanging up. We sent taxis, furniture removers, and fire engines to his door . . . then, as one event tumbled so urgently over another, we forgot him. Baruch, we heard, had been interned in Cyprus. Lennie was a captain in the army.

One day we opened our newspapers and read that Buzz Beurling, Canada's most glamorous war ace, had joined the Israeli air force. That night at Habonim we were told, yes, but the price was a thousand dollars a month. We had out-bid the Arabs.

Beurling never got as far as Eretz. His fighter plane crashed near Rome.

Abruptly, our group began to disintegrate. We had finished high school. Some of the *chaverim* actually went to settle in Eretz, others entered university, still more took jobs. Irving, who had been in charge of our J.N.F. funds, was forced to leave Habonim in disgrace when it was discovered that nearly two hundred dollars was missing.

We made new friends, found fresh interests. Hershey entered McGill. My marks weren't high enough and I had to settle for the less desirable Sir George Williams College. Months later I ran into Hershey at the *Café André*. He wore a white sweater with a big red M and sat drinking beer with a robust bunch of blond boys and girls. Thumping the table, they sang loudly,

> If all the girls were like rabbits,
> and I was a hare I'd teach them bad habits.

My companions were turning out a little magazine. I had written my first poem. Hershey and I waved at each other, embarrassed. He didn't come to my table; I didn't go to his.

Mordecai Richler

SOLOMON GURSKY WAS HERE

Moses Berger, son of the failed poet L.B. Berger, is in the grips of an obsession. The Gursky family with its colourful bootlegging history, its bizarre connections with the North and the Inuit, and its wildly eccentric relations, both fascinates and infuriates him. His quest to unravel their story leads him to the enigmatic Ephraim Gursky: document forger in Victorian England, sole survivor of the ill-fated Franklin expedition and charismatic religious leader of the Arctic. Of Ephraim's three grandsons, Bernard has fought, wheedled and cheated his way to the head of a liquor empire. His brother Morrie has reluctantly followed along. But how does Ephraim's protégé, Solomon, fit in? Elusive, mysterious and powerful, Solomon Gursky hovers in the background, always out of Moses's grasp, but present—like an omen.

"He is a ringmaster, making his performers do dazzling backflips without missing a beat."

Time

"Hilarious, vulgar, dazzlingly well written."

The Globe and Mail

"Beguiling ... malevolently comic ... extravagantly adventurous ... cheerfully misanthropic ... unexpectedly playful, even tender."

The Village Voice

"A big, risky marriage of extravagant comic myth and compelling realism ... a stunning triumph of the imagination."

Maclean's

Norman Levine

SOMETHING HAPPENED HERE

Lean, spare and elegant, these stories by Norman Levine are set in England, France, Zurich and Toronto. The narrator shares with us the subtle nuances of family relationships, love affairs and friendships. From the French ex-officer who befriends the narrator on his trip to Dieppe to the memory of Django Reinhardt and Mon Oncle Antoine in Zurich, *Something Happened Here* is peopled with charming and intriguing characters. This new story collection shows once again that Norman Levine is a writer with a distinctive voice and superb vision.

"[Levine's prose] glows with the honesty and integrity of solid, well-crafted furniture."
The Globe and Mail

Alice Munro

THE PROGRESS OF LOVE

Governor General's Award Winner for fiction
in 1986

With all the ease and mastery that have won extraordinary international acclaim for her writing, the eleven stories in this new collection by Alice Munro invites us into the most intimate moments of human experience—moments of realization about the power, the tenderness and the sacrifice of love.

"One of the year's 10 best fiction books."
New York Times Book Review, 1986

"Moments of insight flash from the pages like lightning."
Philadelphia Enquirer

"Munro's understanding of family life is intricate and profound ... *The Progress of Love* is marvellous."
The Toronto Star

"Alice Munro has earned glowing testimonials for her previous collections of short stories and *The Progress of Love* will bring her many more of them. She deserves them all."
The London Evening Standard

"Alice Munro richly deserves recognition as one of the foremost contemporary practitioners of the short story."
The New York Times

Audrey Thomas

THE WILD BLUE YONDER

This new collection of thirteen stories offers everything that readers have come to love in the writing of Audrey Thomas: a delightful playfulness with language, an affectionate insight into the hearts and minds of women and a clear-sighted vision of the subtleties and ironies of emotional life.

Audrey Thomas's characters emerge from their stories in vivid and often poignant light. In "The Slow of Despond" the thought of returning to Africa with her missionary husband moves a desperate young mother to a tragic act of protection. The remarkable story "Blue Spanish Eyes" is one woman's account of the exhilarating afternoon that utlimately led to her own death. And in the title story a young girl struggles to understand the changes her family undergoes when her father, a World War II pilot, is missing and presumed dead, only to return years later to a world—and a home— which no longer have room for him.

"The wild blue yonder, the laughter and the pain: these are the chosen territories of Audrey Thomas. She navigates them with uncommon skill and bold instincts."

Books in Canada

"Short fiction does not get much better than that sense of startled recognition: of course, you breathe, of course that is what happened."

The Toronto Star

"Thomas is unparalleled in writing about all kinds of culture shock, between strangers from different countries, between lovers of different sexes, between friends with different ideas."

Quill & Quire

Neil Bissoondath

ON THE EVE OF UNCERTAIN TOMORROWS

Neil Bissoondath evokes an exhilarating range of emotions in this expertly crafted collection of short stories. He is a master of comic detail, a sly conjurer of the unexpected, and a compassionate chronicler of people's hopes, fears, dreams and needs.

In the precise and supple prose for which he is renowned, Neil Bissoondath explores the complexities and tragedies, both political and personal, of his vividly created gallery of characters, several of whom do find their tomorrows. Monica in "The Power of Reason" learns a vital and unexpected lesson about the nature of love, Rance in "The Arctic Landscape High above the Equator" struggles with the perils of political loyalty, while Leonard in "Cracks and Keyholes" discovers happiness in a most unpredictable way. In this, his most hopeful book so far, Neil Bissoondath celebrates the small acts of triumph achieved by people emotionally endangered: people searching for a calm centre.

"These tales are a kind of blues for the insomniac, for the emigré, for the restless bird-of-passage."
Independent

"Present and past repeatedly illuminate each other in Bissoondath's stories, and the meaning often comes out of the tension between them ... the best Bissoondath can do is very good indeed."
Books in Canada

"Politically astute, beautifully written, emotionally wrenching and miraculous."

NOW

Timothy Findley

DINNER ALONG THE AMAZON

The sound of screen doors banging, evening lamplight; Colt revolvers hidden in bureau drawers and a chair that is always falling over.

These are the sounds and images that illuminate this brilliant collection of twelve short stories from one of Canada's finest writers.

The stories range from the powerful, haunting "Lemonade", in which a young boy's world is shattered by his mother's self-destruction, to the title story, an unusual journey into the complexities of modern relationships, written especially for this collection.

"Findley writes with uncommon power and skill and with chilling accuracy."
                    The Whig-Standard (Kingston)

"Thanks to this volume, some of the best of Findley's stories are now spread glitteringly before us. His accomplishments in this exacting art are as proportionately large as his novels, as solid as they are brilliant."

                    The Toronto Star

"Each of these stories reveals the passionate intelligence of a major artist."

                    Maclean's

Timothy Findley

STONES

Against a vivid terrain of images, Findley continues his exploration of the many divisive and destructive acts played out on the personal battlegrounds on which we live our daily lives.

From the realities of contemporary relationships to a fantastic vision of urban life; from social comment to the deeply personal—*Stones* is a powerful collection of stories from one of Canada's best-loved writers.

"Break out the champagne: there is a new book by Timothy Findley."
Neil Bissoondath, *The Globe and Mail*

"*Stones* is a masterful performance by Timothy Findley and shed bright, perfect light on a part of that strange, strange thing called the human condition."

The Gazette (Montreal)

"[Findley] has an extraordinary gift for inventing small significant incidents, for entering into other people's personalities and plights and allowing us to see what is both crazy and recognizable about humanity."

The Toronto Star

"Ever elegant, ever precise . . . Findley remains a magical writer . . . magical in the best and truest sense of the word."

The Edmonton Journal